JOHN D. MACDONALD

NOW
DARKER THAN AMBER

A BREATHTAKING NOVEL IN THE TRAVIS McGEE SERIES

Fawcett Gold Medal Books
in the Travis McGee Series
by John D. MacDonald

JOHN D. MacDONALD

DARKER THAN AMBER

FAWCETT GOLD MEDAL • NEW YORK

A Fawcett Gold Medal Book

Published by Ballantine Books

Copyright © 1966 by John D. MacDonald

A shorter version of this novel appeared in Cosmopolitan.

ISBN 0-449-12373-1

Manufactured in the United States of America

First Fawcett Gold Medal Edition: June 1966
First Ballantine Books Edition: July 1982

DARKER
THAN
AMBER

ONE

WE WERE ABOUT to give up and call it a night when some-body dropped the girl off the bridge.

They came to a yelping stop overhead, out of sight, dumped her over the bridge rail and took off.

It was a hot Monday night in June. With moon. It was past midnight and just past the tide change. A billion bugs were vectoring in on us as the wind began to die.

It seemed to be a very final way of busting up a romance.

I was sitting there under the bridge in a skiff with my friend Meyer. We were under the end of the bridge nearest the town of Marathon, and it is the first highway bridge beyond Marathon on your way to Key West —if you are idiot enough to *want* to go to Key West.

My bachelor houseboat, *The Busted Flush,* was tied up at Thompson's Marina in Marathon. It had been there since Saturday afternoon. After I got in I phoned Meyer at Bahia Mar in Lauderdale, where he lives aboard his cabin cruiser. I'd been gone a little longer than I'd planned, and I had one small errand for him to do, and one small apology for him to make for me. I said that in return, if he wanted to come on down to Marathon by bus, I could put him into a good snook hole at the right time of year, tide and moon, and then he could come on back to Bahia Mar with me aboard the *Flush,* and we'd get in late Wednesday afternoon, probably—not that it mattered.

Meyer is the best of company, because he knows when

7

talk is better than silence, and he tries to do more than his share of all the less interesting chores.

Until I asked him to join me, and heard him say yes, I had thought I wanted to be completely alone for a few days.

I'd just finished spending ten days aboard the *Flush* with an old friend named Virginia, known as Vidge. She had come rocketing down from Atlanta, in wretched shape emotionally, trying to find out who she used to be before three years of a sour marriage had turned her into somebody she didn't even like anymore. In the old days she'd never been skyrockets—just a quiet, pretty, decent gal with a nice oblique sense of fun and games, and the manifest destiny of being a good wife.

After three years of Charlie, she was gaunted, shrill, shaky, and couldn't tell you what time it was without her eyes filling with tears. So I took her cruising. You have to let them talk it out. She felt enormous guilt at not being able to make the marriage work. But the more she talked, the more I realized she hadn't had a chance. She was too passive, too permissive, too subdued for an emotional fascist like Charlie. He had leaned too hard. He had eroded her confidence in herself, in everything she thought she was able to do, from meeting people to cooking dinner to driving a car. Finally he had gone to work on her sexual capacities. Were the sexes reversed, you could call it emasculation. People like Charlie work toward total and perpetual domination. They feed on the mate. And Vidge didn't even realize that running away from him had been a form of self-preservation, a way of trying to hang fast to the last crumbs of identity and pride.

At first she talked endlessly, but she couldn't get all the way down to it. She kept saying what a great guy he was and how she had failed him in everything. The third evening, at anchor in a quiet corner of Florida Bay, I managed to get enough of Dr. Travis McGee's truth serum into her. Clean, pure Plymouth gin. By arguing with her, contradicting her, I edged her ever closer to the truth. And in the final half hour, before she passed out, she broke through the barrier and described how much she truly hated that destructive, domineering son of a bitch Charlie. It was very graphic, and she had no idea I was taping it. When she passed out I toted her to the guest stateroom and tucked her in. She slept a little better than around the clock, and was subdued and rueful the next day. That evening she started handing me the Charlie-myth again, and what a failure she was. I played her tape for her. She had hysterics which settled down into a good long hard cry. And after that she was famished enough to eat twenty ounces of rare steak. She slept the clock around again, and woke up feeling that maybe it would be pointless to give the marriage another big try. Vidge and I had a private history of a small affair way back. It would have been better if we had both wanted the same things out of life. But we had kidded ourselves and each other for a time—before reality set in.

The attempt to relive that pleasant nostalgia was a clumsy failure. Charlie had so thoroughly insulted her womanhood she was far too nervous and anxious to be reached. She was certain she had become frigid. I attempted another of Dr. McGee's famous nostrums. I roused her early, and I gave her a full day of swimming, fishing, beachcombing, skindiving and maintenance and housekeeping chores aboard the *Flush*. I gave her a day that would have reminded any marine of boot camp. That night, with the waxing moon at the half, and a good breeze keeping the mosquitoes away from the sun deck, she was too sodden with exhaustion to think of being nervous or anxious or apprehensive when I moved over onto her sun mattress and gently shucked her out of her shorts. She made small purring sounds, half contentment and half sleepy objection. When the sudden awareness that it was working for her brought her wide awake she was too far along to choke herself off with all those anxieties Charlie had built, and when it was done she was happy enough and confident enough to keep chuckling now and again until her breath deepened into sleep.

I lugged her dead weight down to my master stateroom

where, many hours later, in the orange-gold light of the morning sun coming through the curtained portholes, she proved to herself it hadn't been a fluke.

When I put her ashore in Flamingo, she looked two years younger. Her tan was good. She had started to fill out again. Her hands were steady and her voice had lost the edge of shrillness. She smiled to herself quite often. I had gotten her sister on the ship-to-shore through the Miami Marine Operator, and the sister had driven down to Flamingo to pick her up there. I managed to get the sister aside and tell her that if Vidge weakened and went back to Charlie, he might well destroy her completely. The sister, in a calm, dry, unexcited tone, said that if Vidge showed the slightest hint of going back to that monster, she, personally, would giftwrap Vidge and send her back to me in Lauderdale, prepaid. I guess she noticed my alarm at that prospect.

Sure, there had been some pleasure in the missionary work, but dealing at close range with a batch of acquired neuroses can make your ears ring for weeks. She was a good enough memory to set up a gentle nostalgia, but not so great that I would have gone looking for her. Most of all, I think that my nerves were frayed by having to edit everything I said to the lady for the ten days. I was trying to build back some morale and independence, and the wrong comment at the wrong time would have sent Vidge tumbling back down.

You can be at ease only with those people to whom you can say any damn fool thing that comes into your head, knowing they will respond in kind, and knowing that any misunderstandings will be thrashed out right now, rather than buried deep and given a chance to fester.

Vidge, like so many other mild nice people, was a natural-born victim. Life had treated her so agreeably during her first twenty years she'd never had to plant her feet and swing at anything just to maintain her identity. She was loving and giving. And she would have made a delightful permanent package for some guy able to appreciate it. Lots of Vidges never have to find out they're victims. They land with the right people. But when one of them has the bad luck to mate with a Charlie, she gets gobbled up. You see them in the later years, those vague, translucent, silent women who stand over at the edge of life, with the nervous smile that comes and goes, and the infrequent and apologetic cough. Charlie is the squat florid one with the loud laugh and the bright neckties and the scatological jokes and the incipient coronary accident.

Chugging away from Flamingo at low cruise after dropping my passenger, I had the dreary feeling Charlie was going to snare her again and extract double penalties for the little attempt to escape. I was getting oil pressure fluctuation on the starboard diesel, and had a friend in Marathon who would take a look at it without trying to find some plausible way to pick my pocket, so I aimed her in that direction.

My pockets were reasonably hefty. Enough to give me a chance to enjoy another installment of my sporadic retirement. By the end of the year I'd have to dig up a new prospect, somebody so anxious to recover what was legally his that he'd give me half its value for getting it back, half being decidedly better than nothing.

The repair was a minor job, one I could have done myself if I'd been able to diagnose it. I heard the word on the snook hole, remembered the way Meyer would talk a good one up to the side of the boat, and that was how we happened to be under the bridge in a rented skiff Monday midnight, casting the active surface plugs into a splendid snook hole, with the skiff tied to one of the bridge pilings. In the current boil of the incoming tide they had been feeding nicely. I'd had good results with a Wounded Spook with a lot of spinning clattering hardware on it to fuss up the water and irritate them. We'd hooked into at least ten good ones, lost seven amid the pilings, boated three in the eight- to twelve-pound range.

But we were down to that just-one-more-cast. After midnight on a Monday in June, traffic is exceedingly sparse. The concrete bridge span was about twenty feet above the water. We were in the shadows under the bridge. I heard a car coming; it seemed to be slowing down. There was a sudden screech of brakes overhead. And, moments later, the girl came down. She came down through the orange glow of bridge lights and the white pallor of moonlight. Feet first. Pale skirt fluttered upward baring the long legs. Just one glimpse of that, and she chunked into the water five feet off the bow of the skiff, splashing us, disappearing. Motor roared, tires squealed, car rocketed off.

It was a forty-foot drop for her. Twenty feet of air, twenty feet of depth. I would have expected her to bob up but for one thing. She hit my line. The surface plug was a few feet beyond where she hit. And she took it right on down to the bottom, and there the plug stopped taking out line against the drag.

I had twelve-pound mono on that reel. I pulled at it, and it held firm. I tossed my wallet into the bottom of the skiff, shoved my rod at Meyer and asked him to keep the line tight. I yanked my boat shoes off, went over the side, took a deep breath and let half of it out, and pulled myself down the monofilament, hand over hand, sliding my hands along it, grasping it between thumbs and fingerpads. Soon, in the blackness, I reached and touched the hair afloat, dug my fingers into it, got a good hold to try to lift her. Two hands, with that extraordinary gentleness of the last margin of consciousness, closed softly around my wrist. I pulled my way down her body, down to the ankles to find why I couldn't lift her off the bottom. I felt the double ridges of wire biting into the slenderness, leading down and through one of the three oval holes in a hefty cement block. I felt swiftly for the place where it was fastened, felt the hard twist of wire close to the block. I knew that if I had to go up for more air and come back . . . no girl. And my lungs were beginning to try to pump the air in, so that I had to use an effort of will to keep my throat closed against the blind effort. It had been done with pliers. Heavy wire. I knew which way it had to twist. It tore the pads of my thumb and fingers. I hooked fingers into the pocket of my shirt, ripped it off, wrapped it around the wicked ends of the wire, then untwisted as hard as I could. The world was getting a little dreamy. Just slightly vague. But the wire began to unwrap, and the free ends made it easier by giving me more leverage. I wanted to stretch out, yawn, sing some old sad songs, and float on out to sea in the delicious softness of the tide. The wires were free. I yanked them through the hole in the cement block. I kicked hard against the bottom and came slowly up, smiling perhaps, nodding a little, loosely hugging the hips of the drowning girl. I was thrust rudely out of sleepy-bye into the ugliness of coughing and spewing and retching in the fractured moonlight, then trying to hold her so her face was out of the water. That was when I saw Meyer, standing in the skiff, outlined against the lights, carefully playing us two big blundering fish and trying to work us toward the boat. Soon I could help. He knelt and got hold of the girl and worked her aboard over the flat stern, and as I hung on, waiting for strength to climb aboard, I saw him tumble her roughly face down over one of the seats, stand straddling her, reach his hands under her, and pull up slowly, then let her drop and shift his hands and push downward against her back just above the waist.

My feet were beginning to trail outward in the increasing strength of the outgoing tide. Had she been dropped five minutes later I wouldn't have been able to get down to her against that tide run.

I wormed up over the transom, sat there gasping.

"While you were down there," Meyer said, his voice distorted by effort, "I went over to town and had a couple of beers."

"She was alive when I got there, buddy. She grabbed my wrist. So I had to unwire her from her anchor on the first trip."

"Some tenderhearted guy," Meyer said, "didn't have the heart to tell her they were all through. Easier to kill them than hurt their feelings."

"Is that the best way to do that?"

"Shut up. It's my way. And I think it's working."

I fumbled in the tray of the tackle box and found my small flashlight. I'd recently put new batteries in it. Her soaked skirt was bunched, covering her from mid-thigh upward. Quite a pity, I thought, to discard such a long and lovely pair of legs. I rested the flashlight where it shone upon her ankles and hunched down with the fish pliers and nipped the wire. Freed of that stricture the legs moved a little apart, bare feet both turned inward. Bent over in that position, I saw a glitter under the edge of the bunched skirt, reached and lifted it slightly and saw my Wounded Spook against the back of her left thigh, the rear set of gang hooks set deeply. I clipped the leader off it right at the front eyelet, and just as I did so she gave a shallow, hacking cough and spewed water into the bilge, then gagged and moaned.

"Any more criticisms?" Meyer asked.

"What ever happened to mouth-to-mouth?"

"It sets up emotional entanglements, McGee."

After more coughing, she made it clear she wanted no more punishment. Meyer, deft as a bear, rolled her over, scooped her up, placed her in the bow, fanny on the floorboards, shoulders and back against the angle of the gunnels. I put my light on her face. Dark hair was pasted down over one eye. She lifted a slow hand, thumbed the hair back over her ear, squinted, turned her face away from the light, saying, "Please."

I turned the light away, totally astonished to find that it was a face which lived up to the legs, maybe more so. Even in the sick daze of waking up from what could have been that last long sleep, it was delicately Eurasian, sloe-eyed, oval, lovely.

As he moved to reach the lines to free them, Meyer said, "Damned handy, Travis. As soon as you run out, they drop you another one. Stop panting and start the motor, eh?"

TWO

BACK AT THOMPSON'S, I ran the skiff up alongside the starboard stern of *The Busted Flush*. She was tied up with the port side against the pier. While Meyer held it there, I scrambled aboard. He lifted her to her feet, and I reached over the rail, got her, swung her aboard, tried to put her on her feet and had to hold her to keep her from falling. Meyer went chugging off in the skiff to leave it over at the small boat dock where it belonged.

I took her down into the lounge and on through, past the galley to the master stateroom. She stood braced, holding tightly to the back of a chair while I turned the lights on and pulled the pier-side draperies shut. Her head was bowed. She looked up at me and started to say something, but the chattering of her teeth made it unintelligible. I took my heaviest robe from the hanging locker and tossed it onto the big bed, then got her a big towel from the locker in the head and threw it in onto the bed and said, "Get out of that wet stuff and dry yourself good."

I went to the liquor locker, found the Metaxa brandy and poured a good three inches into a small highball glass. I carried it to the stateroom and knocked, and in her chattery voice she told me to come in. She was belting the robe. Her clothing was in a sodden little pile on the floor. I handed her the glass. It chittered against her teeth. She took it down in three tosses, shuddered, then sat on the edge of the bed, hugging herself.

Meyer appeared in the doorway. "Chills? Hmm. Shock. Reaction. Miss, if you have the energy, a hot shower or, better yet, a hot tub. And then another drink. Okay?"

She gave a tense little bob of her head, and Meyer scooped up the wet clothing. In moments I heard the roar of the water into the huge elegant sybaritic tub the original owner had installed to please the tastes of his Brazilian mistress, before I won the vessel from him— sans mistress—in a Palm Beach poker session.

"S-s-s-something . . . in my . . . l-l-l-leg," she said.

I got the needlenose pliers, the good wire cutters, and Dr. Meyer to assist me. We had her lie prone on the giant bed, custom built-in equipment on the boat when I had won her, and Meyer folded the robe back, untangling it from the barbs of the other set of gang hooks on the belly of the speckled plug. I swung the big bed lamp over to bear upon the operating area. There are too many trite words for legs like that. Ivory. Grecian marble. I was considerably more accustomed to brown legs. These had a dusky pallor. But pallor did not mean softness. The chills were in cycles. When a chill tightened her up, the long muscles of calf and thigh, dancer's muscles, swelled—changing the elegant curvatures of those legs in repose. The backs of the thighs and the calves had a fine-grained, flawless, matte finish, and the area of the backs of her knees were shinier, faint blue veining visible under the skin.

We had to adjust our operating technique to the chills, but the brandy was beginning to work, diminishing the violence of them. First, with Meyer steadying the triple shank of the imbedded gang hook, holding it with the needlenose pliers, I nipped through it with the wire cutters, tossed the body of the plug aside. Of the gang hook, two hooks were sunk into her beyond the barb. With Meyer still holding the shank, I clipped the free hook off.

"This is the part that will hurt, dear," Meyer said.

"Go ahead," she said.

There is only one way to remove a fish hook. You have

to push it the rest of the way through, bring the point back out through the skin.

Meyer changed the grip and angle of the pliers, waited for a small chill to end, then made a slow steady twist of his wrist. The two barbed points made two little tents in the skin as they came up from underneath, pushed against the essential toughness, no matter how delicate it may seem, of human hide, then simultaneously pierced through. She made no sound or motion. Wondering if she had fainted, I moved to look at her face. She lay with her eyes open, totally relaxed.

I carefully clipped the barbs off. Bright dark droplets of blood stood out against fairness. I plucked the barbs from the smooth surface of hide, and Meyer, holding the same grip on the pliers, rotated his wrist the other way and brought the barbless curves of metal back out through the channel where they had first dug in. Dab of iodine then, on each of the four small holes, and one round ouchless waterproof patch, size of a half dollar.

"A great honor, Doctor," I said, "to assist you in the technique which bears your name."

Unfolding the back of the robe down over her legs he said, gutturally, "You may haff the object ve remoofed to keep alvays, Kildare."

"Clowns," the girl murmured. "My God."

Meyer hastened out, turned off the bath water. "Your bath awaits, milady. In several minutes I will knock, enter with averted stare, hold the second drink in your direction. The water is very hot. Force yourself into it. What do we call you?"

She sat up slowly, looked in turn at each of us, and her dark eyes were like twin entrances to two deep caves. Nothing lived in those caves. Maybe something had, once upon a time. There were piles of picked bones back in there, some scribbling on the walls, and some gray ash where the fires had been. "Jane Doe will do just fine," she said.

"Your comedy team is Meyer and McGee," he said. "I am Meyer, known as Meyer. The pretty one is McGee, known as Travis, and this is his simple little unassuming houseboat, Jane Doe."

"Delighted," she said, barely moving her lips, and stood up and brushed by us and went into the bath and closed the door.

I went into the guest stateroom which Meyer was occupying. There is a big drawer under the bed. An ironic type had once named it the broad bin, and unfortunately I have been unable to think of anything else to call it. I found girl's pajamas, roomy flannelette in blue and white stripes. I found some black Dacron sailcloth slacks in size twelve, and a white pleated Dacron shirt with long sleeves and with an edge of Dacron lace on the collar and cuffs. I found a pair of zoris that looked about the right size. And I took out one of the little packages, seal unbroken, the better hotels provide for female guests whose luggage has been taken to some highly unlikely place by their friendly airline. The essential toiletries, with a stylized picture of either a blonde or a brunette imprinted on the flexible plastic.

I put them in on the big bed of the boat's owner, debated making the bed up fresh, remembered that the linen had had but one night's use by McGee, and she was not exactly in a condition to be overly fastidious. As I came out of the master stateroom, Meyer came out of the bath after delivering the drink.

"Come take a look," he said. I followed him to the galley. He had drawn a small washtub of fresh water, put her clothing in it to rinse the salt out of the fabric. Mother Meyer.

"What we have, Doctor Watson," he said, "is a raw silk sleeveless blouse in natural color, and an Orlon fleece wraparound skirt, both items with the label of something called, God help us all, The Doll House, in Broward Beach. And we have these lacy little blue briefs, and the matching bra, about a B-cup size 34 I would judge, excellent quality and unlabeled, possibly from a custom house. No shoes. And, as you may have noticed, no jewelry, no wristwatch. But pierced ears, indentation of a ring on the ring finger of the right hand, and though she's no sun bunny, a stripe of pallor on the left wrist where the wristwatch was worn."

I followed him into the lounge. "Age, Mr. Holmes?"

"Some oriental blood. Complicates the problem. I'll say twenty-six, but give me two years either way."

"How about the long decorative fingernails, Mr. Holmes? Too long for useful work, no? And broken practically down to the quick on the third and fourth fingers of the right hand, possibly from a struggle."

"*Very* good, Doctor Watson, my dear fellow. Is there not one other thing worth consideration?"

"Uh . . . the scar on the right cheekbone?"

"Meaningless in itself. Come, man!" I looked blank. He said, "I shall give you a little help, Doctor. Imagine how some other young woman might react to the same set of circumstances."

I thought of Vidge. She wouldn't have endured so placidly the pain of removing the fish hooks. She would have been bleating and hooing and thrashing, and she would have been demanding doctors and policemen. When I said Jane Doe's acceptance of our help seemed significant, he beamed at me and said that her muscle tone, the rich trimness of her figure, her acceptance of the situation all seemed to point to some aspect of the entertainment world, probably one of the more sleazy segments of it, a so-called exotic dancer, a hinterland belly dancer, a bunny at one of the more permissive key clubs, a singer on one of the little cut-rate cruise ships. All her symptoms of near-death had been physical, but emotionally she seemed to have an acceptance of it so placid as to be a little eerie. As if she knew the world as a place where sooner or later they heaved you off a bridge.

We heard a door open, the gargling sound of the tub water running out, the sound of the stateroom door closing. In a few minutes we went as a committee of two, rapped on her door, and heard her call to us to come in. She lay in the middle of the giant bed under the coverings in the striped pajamas, her head, turbaned in a maroon towel, resting on two pillows. Her color had improved. We stood at the foot of the bed. "Much better, eh?" Meyer said.

"I got a little buzz from that big knock of brandy. On account of I guess nothing to eat since breakfast maybe."

"No trouble to fix you something, Jane Doe," I said.

She frowned. "I don't know about solid food. I got a feeling maybe I wouldn't hang onto it so long. Maybe some warm milk and a coupla aspirin, Mr. . . . I forgot your name."

"Travis McGee. The hairy one is Meyer. How about a big warm eggnog with no stick, vanilla, nutmeg on top?"

She looked wistful. "Gee, when I was a little kid . . . sometimes . . . that would be nice, honest." She glanced toward the chair where the clothing was. "There's a girl on board?"

Sometimes when you think you can be casual, it doesn't work at all. When you think something is healed, but then when you least expect it you learn all over again that some things never heal. My voice gave me away when I said, "The girl who owned those clothes is dead."

The normal automatic response would have been to say something about being sorry, but she said, "Then they ought to fit fine. In that big crazy blue tub I was wondering if I was dead, and if you dream things more real-like when you're dead. I guess when I wake up tomorrow I'll know for sure."

"In the morning," Meyer said, "when you feel better, you can tell the whole thing to the police."

Again I was aware of that utter emptiness behind those dark eyes, and of something else back there, a cold and bitter humor, the kind of humor which can make a joke when the hangman adjusts the noose.

"What's to tell?" she said. "I tried to kill myself and it didn't work."

I said, "You tucked that cement block under your arm and hopped over the bridge rail."

"It wasn't easy. You forgot all about the eggnog maybe?"

In an absolutely casual and offhand way, Meyer said something that seemed to be all L's and vowel sounds.

She said, "No, I . . ." She stopped, stared at him with narrow eyes and lips sucked bloodless. "Damn sneaky," she said.

Meyer smiled happily. "Jane Doe from Main Street, Honolulu. Forgive me. I heard just that faintest breath of Island accent in your voice. And you do have that very unique loveliness of the Hawaiian mix, my dear."

"Yah. I'm a dream walking." I have never heard a woman speak of herself with quite that much bitterness.

Meyer turned to me. "Macronesian strains, and add Irish and French and some Japanese and what all, stir for a few generations in a tropical climate and the results can refute the foes of mongrelization." He beamed at the girl. "I'm an economist, my dear. I did a survey of the Islands a few years before statehood, a tax-structure prediction."

You can watch the Meyer Magic at work and not know how it's done. He has the size and pelt of the average Adirondack black bear. He can walk a beach, go into any bar, cross any playground, and acquire people the way blue serge picks up lint, and the new friends believe they have known him forever. Perhaps it is because he actually listens, and actually cares, and can make you feel as if his day would have been worthless, an absolute nothing, had he not had the miraculous good fortune of meeting you. He asks you the questions you want to be asked, so you can let go with the answers that take the tensions out of your inner gears and springs. It is not an artifice. He could have been one of the great con artists of all time. Or one of the great psychiatrists. Or the founder of a new religion. Meyerism.

Once upon a time when Lauderdale was the place where the college mob came in force, I came across Meyer sitting on the beach. He had a half-circle of at least forty kids sitting, facing him. Their faces were alive with delight. Every few minutes there was a big yelp of their laughter. And they were the cold kids, the ones who look at and through all adults exactly the way adults stare at motel art without seeing it. And Meyer was, miraculously, part of that group. When I drifted closer, forty pairs of eyes froze me, and Meyer turned and winked, and I moved along. A kid was playing slow chords on a guitar. Between chords, Meyer would recite. Later I asked him what in the world he'd been doing. He said they were a wonderful bunch of kids. A lovely sense of the absurd. He had been inventing a parody of Ginsberg, entitled "Snarl," making it up as he went along, and he had also made up a monologue of a Barnard girl trying to instill the concept of social significance into the mind of the white slaver who was flying her to Iraq, and he titled that one "The Two Dollar Misunderstanding." Then he had assigned parts to them and brought them into the act, setting the scene up as Richard Burton and Liz Taylor at a White House garden party in honor of culture.

And once I had seen a very reserved matron type, after talking earnestly in a corner with Meyer for three minutes, and without a drink in her, suddenly fall against his barrel chest and sob like a heartbroken child. He would not tell me just what it was that had broken her. His code forbids such revelations, and possibly that is one of his secrets too.

His comfortable little cabin cruiser, named the *John Maynard Keynes,* is tied up a seventy-foot walk from Slip F-18. In the sunset dusk he holds court, with wildly assorted people cluttering the cockpit deck, perching on the rails, sitting on the edge of the dock, legs swinging. And there are always the young popsies, sixteen to twenty, eyes soft with a special worship, content to be near him, the same way those of sterner breed clutter the hotel suites and the pits of the *Grand Prix* race drivers. Were he sensuously unscrupulous he could keep his bunk forever stocked with the exceptional tendernesses of the very young. But, instead, on an average of three times a year he takes unto himself one of that breed which he calls, with warmth rather than irony, the iron maidens. These are stern, mature, aggressive, handsome women who have made their mark in the world, and perhaps forfeited much in the process. Accomplished artists, concert musicians, heads of fashion houses and other competitive businesses, administrators, editors, women in government. He treats them fondly, but as though they are enchantingly foolish young girls, and goes off with his iron maiden of the moment for a few weeks and when he brings them back, their mouths are soft, and their voices have lost that edge of command, and their eyes are filled with that unmistakable look of devotion. When I seemed curious, he suggested I read what Mark Twain had written about choosing a mistress. He said he had discovered just one other factor Twain had overlooked. He said that the woman who achieves a position of power and command is usually so intelligent that she catches on quite quickly when it is explained to her that she has a secret yearning to be hapless and foolish for a little while, to switch off the machinery of domination, to be cherished not only as a woman, but also in the same way she was once cherished when she was a little girl, before she became locked into those motivations that drove her upward so mercilessly. "They want a ribbon in their hair," he explained, "and someone who does not want to make any use of what they've achieved, and someone who would never go around waving their scalp on the end of a spear after they've gone back to the wars, or even look them up at the embassy or in the executive suite someday."

Now he reached and patted Jane Doe's ankle under the sheet and coverlet. "My dear, you are going to have the best sleep you've had in months. Just stay awake long enough for one of McGee's famous eggnogs."

Her smile was almost shy. "Okay."

When I took the eggnog in, she was almost gone, but she stirred, braced herself on an elbow, drank it a few swallows at a time until it was almost gone, looked sleepy-eyed at me and said, "I could be down there dead. And maybe this is the way it would be."

"We're real."

She finished it, handed me the tall glass. "You are. But I don't know about Meyer."

I turned off the light. At the door I said goodnight, but she was already gone. I had heard Meyer come out of the head. He was in the guest stateroom, sitting in lurid pajama bottoms on the side of the bed, digging at the deep, glossy black pelt on his chest.

"She dropped off?" he asked.

"Like tumbling into a well."

"I think you should dispossess me, Captain. I can sleep in the lounge."

"And complain about it for all time? No thanks."

"That was the reaction I hoped for. Look at the time! Ten past two. I've earned my keep. While you were egg-nogging the lass, I went onto the dock, swiftly and deftly filleted the brave snooks, wrapped fillets separately in foil and put them on the second shelf, larger refrigerator, behind the steaks."

"Forgot them completely. Thanks."

"I nearly forgot them, Travis. The lass has a tendency to attract complete attention. Aside from what a delectable morsel she appears to be, what's your reaction to her?"

I leaned against a built-in stack of drawers, arms folded. "Wariness, I guess. Like they say about stalking a panther, you're never sure of who's after who. A hell of a lot of control there, Meyer. I think it looked like a very professional job of trying to kill her. No husband discarding the tiresome wife. So somebody had to have a very good reason for scuttling merchandise of that quality. She must have given them enough reason. And they didn't make it easy for her. No rap on the skull before they chunked her over. I can guess she's really shook, but she's not going to let herself show it in any way. Or yell cop. She's a hard one, Meyer. I get the impression of . . . gambler's nerves. She took a chance and lost. She accepted the loss and knew what it would mean. Then got a break she had no right to expect. I detect the smell of money. And she was playing in a rough league."

Meyer sighed. "I think we'll get some answers from her, if she thinks there's any way she can use us. Partial answers probably. I noticed one thing. Any girl that attractive almost always has dozens of little automatic tricks, a way of looking at a man, speaking to him, holding herself. Not so much flirtatiousness as awareness of the weapons she's always owned, and how to use them at all times. I've been trying to think of the categories I've run into where they can turn the whole arsenal on and off at will. Good trained nurses, dedicated actresses, ballet dancers'. . . and whores. And we won't know why those two men dropped her off that bridge unless she decides it is in her best interests to tell us."

"Two men?"

"At least two, and probably in a convertible. From the time the car braked to a stop until she hit the water, there wasn't time to work her out of a sedan with that block wired to her ankles, and I doubt they'd have her strapped to a fender like a dead doe. And also there was no sound of a car door at any time. The car started up so quickly, whoever dropped her wouldn't have had time to get back behind the wheel. Besides, the motor was being revved the whole time it was stopped. So I see a nervous man at the wheel and a powerful man in the back seat with her. Powerful and agile. He jumped out over the door, scooped her up—a hundred and twenty pounds of girl plus cement block—swung her up and over the parapet and let her drop feet first, vaulted back into the car as the other man started it up. I'd also guess they were parked a distance from the bridge, lights out, well over on the shoulder, waiting to be certain nothing was coming from either direction. As she knew what was going to happen, it must have been a horrid wait for her. But I would wager she didn't whine or beg."

I shook my head admiringly. "Ever wonder if you're in the wrong line of work, Professor?"

"I'm in the logic business, McGee. I deduce possibilities and probabilities from what I can observe. My God, man, compared to the mists and smokes of economic theory and practice, the world of actual events seems almost oversimplified. A corporate financial statement is the most nonspecific thing there is. If a man can't read the lines between the lines between the lines, he might as well stuff his money into a hollow tree."

In that villain's face the eyes are an intense blue, bracketed by the wrinkles of weather and smiling, small eyes peering from either side of the potato nose. "Don't overrate my talents, boy. You function superbly in areas where I'd be helpless as a child. I couldn't have gone down after her, or made myself stay down when I learned it was the only way to save her."

"McGee, all meat and reflexes."

"And illusion. One of the last of the romantics, trying to make himself believe he's the cynical beach bum who has it made. You permit yourself the luxury of making moral judgments, Travis, in a world that tells us man's will is the product of background and environment. You think you're opportunistic and flexible as all hell, but they'd have to kill you before they could bend you. That kind of rigidity is both strength and weakness."

"Aren't you swinging a little wild tonight, Prof?"

He stuck a fist against a huge and shuddering yawn. "I guess so. A funny hunch that Miss Jane Doe is very bad news. And I've seen how you take on problems. You get deeply involved. You bleed a little. Indignation makes you take nutty risks. All that splendid ironic detachment goes all to hell when you detect a dragon off in the bushes somewhere. I wouldn't want you to get the same professional kind of attention she got. I'd miss you. Where would I find another pigeon who gets clobbered by the queen's gambit? Or knows how to lead Meyer to the fat snook. Good night, pigeon."

After I had made my nest on the big yellow couch in the lounge and put the lights out, I forgave Meyer for prodding me with his parlor psychology. He'd depicted me as a little too much of a gullible ass. Sometimes, sure, I'd identified a little too closely with a customer, and when you couldn't help them, it could leave a lasting bruise. But I have been there and back time after time, and had my ticket punched. No matter how much I despised the fat cats who devise legal ways of stealing, I had learned not to give them any odds-on chances of puncturing the brown hide of McGee. It had happened enough times to teach me that in spite of the miracles of modern medicine, hospitals are places where they hurt you, and that when you hurt enough the cold sweat rolls off you and the world goes black. I knew I had some parts nobody could replace if they got smashed, and once deep in the wormy comfort of the grave there would be no chance to identify with the gullible ones, nor any chance to nip in and snatch the meat out of the jaws of the fat cats.

The dead-eyed cookie was not likely to elicit any warmth and sympathy from the McGee, nor send him off in any galumphing charge to recover the magic grail. Besides, I had enough bread for months of joyful leisure, for cruising, beachcombing, getting happily plotzed with good friends, disporting with the trim little jolly sandy-rumped beach kittens, slaying gutsy denizens of the deep blue, and slipping the needle into every phony who happened into my path. When it came time to embark on the next profitable crusade, it would be for the sake of someone considerably more helpless than our Eurasian Jane Doe.

But those certainly were fantastic legs.

THREE

I STARTED mousing around the galley early, certain both boat guests were asleep. It startled me when Meyer came aboard. He came onto the stern deck and knocked softly on the lounge door. I went and opened it for him.

"Lock yourself out? Why?"

"For the same reason I got up and buttoned the whole boat up after you'd sacked out last night. I started wondering if anybody could have stayed on the bridge to make sure she stayed down. Not likely. But it's not a bit of trouble to lock up."

"Where have you been, Meyer?"

"A morning stroll. The view from the bridge. About two miles there and two miles back. That adds up to a six-egg breakfast. I wanted to confirm some guesses."

"Such as?"

"It sounded to me as if they took off in the direction of Miami. The tire marks check out. They swerved over onto the wrong side of the bridge to jettison their sweet cargo. Skid marks. And then more skid marks where they scratched off and swerved back into their own lane. They stopped fairly near this end of the bridge, and it has enough center rise so they couldn't see the road behind them while stopped. But from the top of the rise you have a good straight shot for about four miles south. And, from where they dumped her over, you can see a good mile straight ahead. With their lights out, nobody coming from the direction of Marathon would notice them on the wrong side of the bridge. But they had to know it would be clear enough. So I walked further and, about two hundred yards south of the bridge, the shoulder is so wide you can park there and see *around* the bridge. Tires had mashed the grass down." He took an object from his shirt pocket, a very generous cigar butt, better than three inches long, wrapped in a tissue. He held it on the palm of a big paw, prodded it with a thick hairy finger. "We had a good rain about eight last night, remember? This hasn't been out in the rain. Looks like a very good leaf. From where I found it, right at the edge of the brush, the passenger threw it out. I don't think you could throw a cigar that far from a car on the highway proper. And this isn't the kind you throw away. The wet grass put it out. You don't throw it away unless you've lit it to settle your nerves, and then somebody says let's go, and you have a girl to dump over a bridge railing in the next minute. Then you throw away a good cigar. Nice teeth marks, Travis. Big choppers. They'll stay nice and clear even after this has dried out all the way. So would you humor an aging economist and tuck it away in a good safe place? One of us might meet the fellow again."

He rewrapped it carefully and I accepted it. "Anything else, Inspector?"

"Ah yes. As an ignorant tourist I queried a surly old fellow about water depths. Except in the main channel under the center of the bridge, most of the rest of the area averages about three feet at low tide. One exception, the hole where we were fishing, where the outgoing tide sets up a good swirl. Fifty feet in diameter, twenty and thirty feet deep. The highway people worry about it undercutting some of the bridge piers eventually. Over the main channel the bridge walls are considerably higher, too high to conveniently hoist a girl over. So either the man with the cigar, or the fellow racing the engine, or perhaps a third man if there was one, knows the waters hereabouts. In fact, dear heart, there might be other cement blocks down there, with empty loops of wire. When the crabs and the other scavengers have picked them clean, the ligaments would rot and the bones separate at the joints. The slender bones of the leg would slip out of the loops as soon as the feet were gone, and it would not make much difference by then, I imagine. We may have discovered the southeastern repository for surplus bawds. That fatal ka-slosh on many a dark night, my boy. And the slow empty dance of the tethered bawds in the final caress of the current deep and black, the wild hair drifting, and the aimless sway of their emptied arms, and the slow oceanic tilting of their sea-cool hips in the . . ."

"Meyer! At eight in the morning?"

"Extreme hunger gives me poetic delirium. Travis, good lad, you look unwell."

"I was, for a moment. You see, Meyer, I was down there. And it was black. And when I wound my fist in her hair to try to lift her, and found I couldn't, she was just enough alive to reach up and put both hands on my wrist, as gently as a sick child. If she hadn't done that, I wouldn't have been able to stay down long enough to get her loose. Yes, Meyer, it was deep and black. And not very nice."

"I am often guilty of vulgarity. Forgive me. Have we a nice mild onion I can chop into my six scrambling eggs?"

We were on second coffees when we heard her running the water in the head. Soon she appeared in the doorway, looking down at us in the booth adjoining the stainless steel galley, wearing the black pants and the white shirt with its trimmings of lace.

"Goodmorning to Meyer and McGee," she said. "If there is really no other woman aboard, one of you is a perfect jewel, washing out the dainty underthings."

"Always at your service, Miss Doe," Meyer said. He got up. "Sit here, my dear. Opposite the McGee. Boat owners get waited on hand and foot. I'm chef as well as laundress. And your turn will come. Coffee black and hot first?"

"Please." She slid rather stiffly into the booth, grimaced as she lowered herself.

"How do you feel?" I asked her.

"As if somebody had tried to break my back."

As he placed the coffee in front of her, Meyer said, "Thank me for that too. I stretched you out across a boat seat and I could feel your ribs give every time I pushed the air out of your lungs. But I was reasonably careful not to break any."

The morning light was brilliant against her face as she sat opposite me. Her dark hair was brushed to a gloss, hung free, two dark curved parentheses which framed the lovely oval of her face, swung forward as she dipped her head and lifted the cup to her lips. She had made up her mouth carefully with the lipstick from the convenience kit. The pale down on her face, just below the darker hair of the temples, grew quite long. There was one faint horizontal wrinkle across the middle of her forehead, twice arched to match the curve of her brows. And a slightly deeper horizontal line across her slender throat. A few pores were visible in the ivoried dusk of her skin where it was taut across the high solidity of oriental cheekbones, but there was no other mark or flaw upon her, except the cheekbone scar shaped like a star. In that light the color of her eyes surprised me. Light shrunk the pupils small. The irises were not as dark as I had imagined. They were a strange yellow-brown, a curious shade, just a little darker than amber, and there were small green flecks near the pupils. Her upper lids had that fullness of the Asiatic strain, and near-death had smudged the flesh under her eyes. She looked across at me and accepted the appraisal with the same professional disinterest with which the model looks into the camera lens while they are taking light readings.

"And otherwise?" I asked.

She lifted her shoulders slightly, let them fall. "I slept fine. You men will have to fill in some blanks. Where are we?"

"Tied up at Thompson's Marina at Marathon."

"And last night, after I corked off, did you dear boys go honking and blustering over to the beer joints to make the big brag about what you rescued from the briny?" Her voice was mild, but there was a curl to her lips.

Meyer smiled down at her. "I don't know how McGee

reacts to that, my dear, but personally I find the inference offensive. How would you like how many eggs?"

"Uh . . . two. Easy over."

"With a little slab of sautéed fish? And a quarter of one of Homestead's better cantaloupes?"

"Yes. . . . Yes, please. Mr. Meyer?"

"Just Meyer."

"Okay. Meyer, I'm sorry I said that. It's just that I'm a little spooked."

"Forgiven," Meyer said. "We bluster, dear. We bluster all to hell and gone. But honk? Never!"

Meyer served her, poured us both more coffee, then came and wedged in beside me with his own cup.

"I don't know how you saved me," she said.

Meyer explained it all, how we happened to be there, what we saw and heard, and who had done what. As he explained, she ate with a delicately avid voracity, a mannerly greed, glancing up at Meyer and at me from time to time.

"McGee stayed down just long enough to make my blood run cold," Meyer said. "I know it was better than two minutes."

She looked at me, eyes narrowing slightly in a speculation I could not read. I said, "I knew you were alive when I got to you. So that was the only good chance I had to bring you up alive, to get you loose that first time."

"And you heard the car leave?"

"Before you touched bottom," I said.

Her plate was empty. She put her fork down with a little clink sound. "Then we three, right here, are the only people who know I'm alive. Right?"

"Right," said Meyer. "Our plans before you . . . uh, excuse me, dropped in . . . were to leave sometime this morning and head for Miami. Want to come along?"

She shrugged. "Why not?"

"My dear," Meyer said, "it would seem as if someone took a violent dislike to you last night."

"Is that a question?"

"Only if you want to give an answer. We are not

going to pry. So you don't have to make up any answers. Tell us what you feel like telling us, or nothing at all."

"He . . . one of them—there were two—he didn't like it. He wished there was some way to get around it, so it wouldn't have to happen. But he knew and I knew we were way past any place where there was any chance of turning back. I was scared sick. Not of dying. When you take a chance and lose, that's the chance you take. What he didn't like most was being told not to make it easier. He didn't think that was right. And that's what had me so scared, going out the hard way. Being down in the water and no chance to do anything, and holding my breath down in the dark on the bottom as long as I could. I whispered to him, begging him to put me out first. He knows how. I thought he would. He could have done it so Ma . . . so the other one wouldn't even have heard. But then they stopped and as he swung me over, that wire hurting me terrible, and let me go, I knew he wasn't going to." She stopped and gave us both a look of savage satisfaction. "I was taking a breath to scream my lungs out but then I knew that if I didn't make a sound, the other guy would think Terry had hit me on the throat before dumping me, and he'd have to report it, and they might give him a hard time. I sure owed him a hard time, so I didn't let myself make a squeak and it . . . I guess it took my mind off everything a little bit, and at least I ended up down there with a big hunk of air in my lungs instead of all screamed out. Funny, it could have made the difference."

"And probably did," Meyer said. "And it was why I thought someone was disposing of a dead body, the way you came down without a sound. A good thing Travis got down there quickly."

"Boy, if they ever find out somebody got me up in time!" I saw her shiver. It was a clue to her being more rattled than she would let herself show us. Her voice was at odds with her pale and dusky elegance. It was a rich, controlled contralto, but she switched back and forth from the vulgarity of an artificial elegance of expression to a forthright crudeness. I could not tell

whether it was spirit or stupidity that made her feel
pleased with her own cleverness in giving Terry a hard
time as she was, as far as she knew, being murdered.

She raised her eyebrows in surprise and said, "You
know, I haven't even said thanks! Okay, thanks guys.
McGee, I say it took guts to go down there after me,
and it was a nice thing to do for anybody. I don't remember much. Just all black and terrible, and then somebody pulling my hair and touching me, maybe a fish
going to eat me. Then being in all that fish smell, and
somebody pushing at me, and heaving up that water all
over. So here I am. And thanks."

"You are most welcome," Meyer said. "And here you
are, with a second life to lead. Everything since last night
is pure profit. So what are you going to do with your
new life?"

The question seemed to alarm her. "I don't *know*!
I haven't had to think of things like that. I've always
been *told* what to do, and brother I better do it. I don't
want to have to *think* about what I should do." She
bit her lip and looked at each of us in turn, head
slightly tilted. "You boys look like you've got something
going for you. I mean, this boat and all, and you have a
lot of cool. It's not a fishing trip and back to the old
lady and the office. If you've got something going, maybe
there's some kind of way I could fit into things."

It was touching in an inverted way. The family had
moved away, leaving the housecat to scratch at a new
screen door.

"I'm an economist, just as I told you, my dear, and
McGee here is in the salvage business, on contract."

"It's squarer than I thought," she said wistfully. "Maybe
no matter what I work out, it is going to get back to
those people I'm walking around, and they'll try again.
They can't miss twice."

"If you're looking for advice," Meyer said, "we can't
give you any without knowing the problem, Miss Doe."

"Vangie," she said. "I owe you at least my right name,
huh? Short for Evangeline. The whole name will kill
you, honest. Evangeline Bridget Tanaka Bellemer. Bel-

lemer is sort of French meaning beautiful sea. That's a gas! That's what I got dropped into—the beautiful sea. I guess I have to settle down and think things out somehow. When do we get to Miami? After lunch?"

It amused me. "Maybe by five or six tomorrow evening."

She looked relieved. "I wish it was next month, or next year. Anyway, there's more time than I thought, and that's a help."

"Ask for advice if you think you need it," Meyer said. "And you look well enough to accept a temporary appointment as dishwasher."

She stared at him. "Are you *kidding*!"

"On this vessel," I said, "everybody works."

"I'm not so big on housework," she said with a trace of sullenness mixed with acceptance of her fate.

After I'd settled the bill for dockage and fuel, Meyer handled the lines and I ran the *Flush* out of there, sitting up at the topside controls forward of the sun deck. When we were out into the channel Meyer went below. In a little while she came up and asked permission to sit in the co-pilot seat. She had found a white shirt of mine and put it on over the borrowed blouse. She had found a hat left aboard by a guest, a straw thing with cute sayings on it and a floppy brim a good yard in diameter. She had found some sunglasses. She had a tall highball in hand, almost as lethally dark as iced coffee.

"Okay I made myself a knock?" she asked. "Want I should go get you one too?"

"Later on, maybe. Won't you be too warm?"

"It's not so bad now, with the wind. What the sun does to me, I break out. Like little boils. So I have to watch it. You know, Meyer is pretty fussy, isn't he? I washed the damn dishes. He said I left grease on, I should wash them again. I said once was all I bargained for, so he's down there washing them all over. Gee, I can see how come it takes so long to Miami. This thing is *really* slow."

"But cozy."

"What it's like, Travis, is a real great apartment pad, the hi fi and furniture and all. You could fill it with swingers and really blast away."

She was quiet for a long time. She was not exactly killing her drink. Tiny sips were widely spaced. I was aware of her examining me from time to time, long glances behind the dark lenses.

"Look, in this salvage business, I suppose it's like other kinds of things, there's a contract you want to get and a lot of people want to get it too because there's good money in it. In business you do better if you have some kind of an edge, right? Maybe what would be a help to you, I was thinking, some way to soften up those guys, so they want to have you do the work. What you could do, maybe, is put the price a little higher, to cover whatever it would cost to make them feel friendly."

"Sorry, honey. It doesn't work that way."

More silence. We passed a bar where about forty pelicans stood in single file in about an inch of water. I pointed it out to her and she said, "Yeah. Birds." Most people are as blind as Vangie. Eyesight is what you use to get around without running into things. But they find no aesthetic value in what they see.

Her drink went down, a little bit at a time. Suddenly she started questioning me about my houseboat. I really owned it? Could I take it any distance? Could I get it over to New Orleans, or maybe Galveston? Did I get to use it often, or was I too busy with my salvage business? Costs something to run such a nice boat, huh? Don't lots of people charter their boats to get some of their bait back? A boat like this, did you ever think there could be a way to turn it into a real gold mine? Like sort of little weekend excursions, with everything done real tasty.

I finally realized what she had in mind. She couldn't risk staying in the Miami area. But if I could cruise to other waters, she'd help me get set up in the excursion business. She'd line up three or four fun kids, hire a cook and a maid, stock up with steaks and champagne and offer weekend excursions for the tired businessman at a thousand dollars a head. "Out of just three pas- sengers, you could net better than a grand, McGee, be- lieve me."

"Until somebody drops us both off a bridge, Vangie?"

"Come *on*! I was messed up in something a lot rougher than *that*. I should have known when I was well off, back when I was just a plain ordinary hustler. So I had to go and let myself get talked into this . . . this other kind of work. Most of the time I didn't let it bother me. But once in a while, one of the johns would be different. Sweet, sort of. And then I'd think he should get a better deal than what he was going to get. It seemed too raw. And so . . . hell, I had a couple of drinks and got soft and hinted what was going to happen to him. I could have ruined the whole setup for every- body. But they got to him before he could get to the law, and that was that. But I was finished. They didn't dare use me anymore, and couldn't trust me not to fink on them if they cut me out of the action, so the only thing they could do was take me off the books for good. I knew that. I guess I blew it because I think my nerves had been going bad. You work a setup like that long enough and you begin to dream about those guys and what happened to them all. And you begin to imagine people are following you. If I hadn't tried to tip that one off, it would have been the next one or the one after that. Look, you don't buy the cruise boat idea, huh?"

"No thanks. Vangie, what kind of a setup were you in?"

"If you don't know, you stay healthy. What I ought to do is blow the whistle on the whole group. But it would be a terrible thing to do to the other two gals who got pressured into it just like I did. I think they'll crack sooner or later too. Anyway, the law could get so excited about it maybe I couldn't make any kind of a deal anyway. When somebody lifts the lid off the pail of worms, it's going to get very very warm for everybody, and you can believe it. What I keep thinking, I haven't been a blonde since I was seventeen, and quit when my hair started cracking and splitting. There's some money

I can pick up if I can get to it, if they haven't staked it out. I could get a nose job too, maybe, or something around the eyes they do to change you. And I heard if you make the right contacts, you can get set up pretty good in Australia lately. The bad thing is how . . . everybody's getting nervous."

"Why?"

"Because it's been going on so long. You get the feeling the odds are going bad. Because they're nervous, if they grab me again, they'll take it out on me for scaring them by getting away. They'll make me beg to be back down in that water wired to a rock."

Meyer appeared to hand me my eleven o'clock bottle of chilled Tuborg. She turned toward him and said, "You sore or anything?"

"Should I be?"

"Maybe you should. But it's kind of a thing with me, Meyer. I was in a Home for a while, and I had to do every kind of scut work there was and I swore I wouldn't ever again, even if I had to use food money for maid service."

He moved around her and leaned against the rail. We talked. He asked gentle questions. She finished her drink at last and went below and came back with another just as tall and just as dark. I suspected that her nervousness about her future had been making her increasingly talkative with me. And the beginning of the second drink unfastened her tongue a little more. She began to try, quite obviously, to shock Meyer out of his placid and friendly acceptance of her, and in doing so gave us enough clues and false clues so we could fit together a coherent and plausible history. Her brothers had been blown up while playing on a Hawaiian beach, had dug up something that went off. After the war her mother had brought the six-year-old Vangie to the States. Her mother had come to track down the Navy officer who had promised to divorce his wife and marry Vangie's mother. The officer brushed her off. Her mother found waitress work, acquired a brutal boyfriend. By the time Vangie was ten she was unmanageable in school. When they threatened to send her to an institution for delinquent children she called their bluff by becoming so shamelessly delinquent they had to send her away. After she had been in the institution two years, a truck crushed her mother to death against the back wall of the restaurant where she worked. At thirteen, looking almost eighteen, she seduced the resident director of the institution and blackmailed him into taking her off all menial work and giving her special food and privileges. Over a year later somebody reported the situation to the state attorney general's office, and the director, to save his own neck, smuggled her out and turned her over to a vice ring working the Virginia Beach area. They beat all rebellion out of her. She was transferred to other stations on the national circuit, and by the time she was twenty-four she was working for a call circuit in Jacksonville and making the top dollar in the area. Two years ago she had been recruited into the dangerous game she would not describe.

Certainly the breaks had gone against her. Circumstance had turned her into an emotional basket case. You could bleed a little for the Hawaiian child who couldn't comprehend what had happened to the big brother who had carried her around on his shoulders.

The Busted Flush droned roughly east by northeast up the channel in the midday glare. I'd pulled my T-shirt off and I was slumped back in the big topside pilot seat, squinting to pick up the familiar markers, steering by means of bare toes braced against a top spoke of the wheel. Swathed against the sun, shadowed by the huge hat, Miss Vangie talked on and on in that creamy contralto, Meyer braced nearby, beaming and nodding, a devoted audience.

She lunged back and forth through time, with side trips into obvious fantasy and self-delusion, her mode of speech changing from imitation duchess elegance to clinical crudity. All the basic patterns emerged, the way a design will appear after the etcher has made his ten thousand tiny gravings on the copper plate. Perhaps some social psychologist would have given his chance of an honorary degree to have the whole rambling recital on tape. It was interesting in the beginning. I guess any normal person has curiosity about the inner structure of organized prostitution, the dangers to avoid, the payoffs, the mechanics of solicitation, the ways of extracting extra bounty when they get hold of a live one.

But after a time it was repetitious and dull. Too much detail about the furnishings of darling apartments, about the accumulation of darling wardrobes. The life of a sandhog tunneling under a river can be fascinating until you have to listen to a play-by-play of every shovel load of muck. And so when Meyer went below to fix lunch, and she decided she was maybe getting too much sun through reflection off the water and followed him down, the silence was welcome.

In the silence I tried to sort her out. Her twelve years on the track had coarsened her beyond any hope of salvage. Though I know it is the utmost folly to sentimentalize or romanticize a whore, I could respect a certain toughness of spirit Vangie possessed. She had not howled as she fell to her death. She had not flinched or murmured as we cut the hooks out of her leg. And she had bounced back from the edge of death by violence with remarkable buoyancy. The talking jag seemed the only symptom of how shaken she had been. I could think of few women I had known who could have taken such terror in stride.

I realized I felt proud of her. This reaction was so irrational it startled me. I tracked it down to its obvious source. It was the inevitable sense of ownership. I remember talking all night long to a damned fine surgeon. At one time during the night he spoke of the ones he had hauled back through those big gates when he had no right to expect it could be done. "They become your people," he said. "Your kids. You want the good things for them because they get it on time you gave them. You want them to use life well. When they crap around, wasting what you gave them, you feel forlorn. When they use it well, you feel great. Maybe because it's some kind of a ledger account, and they have to make up for what those others would have done, those ones you lost for no damn good reason."

I knew that the risk I'd taken had been for the sake of putting another hooker back on the tiles. So I had to believe she had enough essential spirit and toughness to be able to make it some other way, and would.

FOUR

AT THREE-THIRTY, after Vangie had sacked out, the wind changed, moving in our direction, making it so hot at the topside controls I had Meyer take the wheel while I strung a tarp for shade. Then we sat and talked about our passenger, agreeing that the talking jag was reaction hysteria.

"Also," Meyer said, "she has to level with us. She can't help adding trimmings, but it is essentially true. Maybe she didn't want to tell a pair of civilians about her career. Maybe she wanted to pretend to be something else. But if she'd pretended to be something else, how would that work when we get to Miami? Say she was going back to the model agency? Back to the husband and kiddies? Back to the old secretarial desk? By leveling she's asking for help and advice. How does she get out of the range of the people who'll take another try at her?"

"But without leveling all the way."

I had told him about that part of the conversation he hadn't been there to catch. "Travis, she keeps walking around it, getting a little closer every time. I think she *wants* to tell us. I think she *wants* to get it off her chest. Whatever she's been doing for the past two years, it makes her feel guilty. But she has a real dilemma. If she tells us enough so we can tip off the authorities, her girlfriends will suffer right along with the men in the group. Even so, if we stay receptive, I think she'll get around to it, just in the forlorn hope we'll be able to tell her what to do."

"Got any guesses about what she's been doing?" I asked.

Impatiently he said, "You listened to her, just as I did. Blackmail doesn't upset her. Nor does conspiracy, nor theft, nor extortion, nor addiction, nor mayhem. Let's say there aren't many choices left."

"At least it upset her."

"Yes indeed. After two years, it began to make her edgy."

Tarpon Bay seemed a reasonable halfway point, and after I had moved well off east of the channel, set the big hook in good bottom and killed the engines, she came stretching and yawning up into the sunset light to say that it looked as if we were in a lake, and why were we stopping, was it busted?

I explained that we didn't want to overtax the captain by running all night, so parking was standard operating procedure.

As it was very still and very hot, I got the big auxiliary generator going, and we buttoned up the boat and put the airconditioning on high. The fading day put an orange-gold light through the starboard windows of the lounge. I briefed her on the music machinery, and after she couldn't find anything she liked among my tapes or records, I put the FM tuner into the circuit and she prowled the band from end to end until she settled for a Hollywood station whanging away at what Meyer terms beetle-bug mating chants. She boosted the bass and put the gain slightly below torture level. My big amplifier fed the rackety-bang into the big wall-mounted AR-2a stereo speakers, giving us all the resonances and overtones from twenty cycles all the way up to peaks no human ear can detect.

I had let her dig into the broad bin. She had left it open, of course, with a strew of discards on the floor nearby, just as she left any empty glass at the place where she finished it, hung the clothes she took off on the floor, left the bourbon bottle uncapped on the galley countertop, cluttered the head with toiletries, lipsticked the towels, left dark hairs in the basin. Though indifferent to all the spoor she left behind her, she spent all the time she was not talking, eating or sleeping in tidying herself. She put in a fantastic amount of mirror time, and was delighted to find a little kit in the broad bin which gave her the chance to work with great concentration on fingernails and toenails, filing the broken fingernails carefully. In the most unlikely event she was ever aboard for a longer cruise, I knew I would have to ration the showers she took. She would strain the capacity of even the oversize fresh water tanks aboard the *Flush*.

Digging through the broad bin she had come up with short brown shorts in a stretch fabric and a sleeveless orange blouse which she did not button, but had overlapped before tucking it into the shorts so that it fitted her torso very trimly. Barefoot, she danced alone on the lounge carpeting, half of a dark drink in her hand. The dance was mildly derivative of the frug-fish-watusi, moving to a new place, facing in a new direction from time to time. Meyer and I had dropped the desk panel and we sat on either side of it, playing one of those games of chess where, by cautious pawn play by both of us, the center squares had become intricately clogged as the pressure of the major pieces built up, and each move took lengthy analysis. While he pondered, I watched Vangie. She gave no impression of being on display. Her face was without expression, eyes partially closed. She rolled and twisted her body to the twang-ka-thump music, but in a controlled and moderate way. I could not tell if she was lost in the music or lost in thought. Nearly everyone over nineteen who tries the modern dances of the young looks so vulgar as to be almost obscene. And I would have expected Evangeline to be no exception.

But when she bowed her head, the wings of dark hair swung forward, and in the rhythmic turning of her upper body from side to side, in the roll and swing and cadence of her hips, she achieved that curious quality of innocence the young ones project, wherein body movements that are essentially sexual become merely symbolic sexual references, mild and somehow remote.

I knew she had no awareness of our watching her from time to time. I tried to identify the factors that enabled her to project that special flavor. The brief shorts enhanced the length and grace and elegance of her legs. The way she had overlapped the blouse made it loose across the bosom, blurring her contours. Part of the effect was due to the restraint of her movements. But in large measure it had to be the shape of her in waist, flanks, hips, thighs, buttocks. There was a look of fullness and ripeness, but all of it trimmed by the interwoven musculature under that thin subcutaneous fat layer that makes the softness of woman. There was no loose wobbling, no saddlebag pads of flesh above the hips, no softness of waist, no jounce of inner thigh or sag of belly. There was a tilt of that flatness just below the last knuckles of the spine, that flat place where there are two dimples in healthy flesh, and below that the buttocks swelled into a solid roundness, without droop or flaccidity. Then it was the tightness of the flesh of youth that must give these dances their curiously somber quality, a brooding, inward look to those earthy movements. When the flesh is taut, the dance becomes strangely ceremonial. It is a rite that celebrates the future, and it was eerie to see how accurately it could be imitated by a woman who had left any chance of love so far in the past.

When it was my move, I saw that Meyer had not, as I had expected, begun the disruption of the balance of power in the center squares. He had moved a bishop, bringing more force to bear. As I began to study it, he went away and came back bearing what he calls his tourist disguise, a huge black camera gadget bag. He put it down, bent over it and pawed around and selected a Nikon F body and a medium telephoto lens.

He turned the palm of his hand to catch the same light that was on her face, and took a meter reading from his palm. He set speed and aperture, went down onto one knee, focusing with the lens aimed upward toward her. The clack of the reflex mechanism was muffled by the music. He moved to a new angle, caught her again and again, unaware, until she turned in her solitary ritual and saw him and stopped and said, "Oh, come *on!*"

"Strictly amateur," he called to her over the din of music. "Dead fish, broken sea shells, old stone walls, lovely faces."

"But here's what you *want*, Meyer, for God's sake," she said. She shook her dark hair back, turned at an angle to him, wet her lips, arched her back, then stood hipshot, head lowered, eyes hooded, lips apart, staring into the lens with stylized lustful invitation.

She struck three such poses and Meyer recorded them dutifully, but I knew he had no interest in that kind of record. When he thanked her and put the camera away, she went over and turned the volume down and said, "I posed for a lot of art model stuff, you probably saw it in girlie magazines, except I haven't done any the last two years. I've got such a good body, the way it photographs, I got pretty good money, but let me tell you it's harder work than you'd think. It worked out pretty good as something to keep some money coming in when we got the word to knock off for a couple of weeks, and another thing, when you tell the fuzz you're a model, and you've got the glossies and the magazines to prove it, they better believe it."

Meyer had returned to the chess game. She left the music turned down, went and built herself a new drink and came back and stared at the board as I made a pawn-takes-pawn move that would force a recapture and open up the middle squares.

"Maybe," she said, "instead of that dumb game you boys could stake me twenty for a start and we could play three-way gin. Quarter of a cent? You'd get my marker for the twenty and I never faulted on a marker in my life, you can believe it."

"Maybe later," Meyer said.

"Excuse me all to hell," Vangie said, turned up the music and went back to her dance, pausing to take her tiny sip of the drink from time to time.

That night I was back in an old dream, asleep on the yellow couch in the lounge, the airconditioning off, the *Flush* unbuttoned, a faint coolness of night breeze moving through the screening of the open hatches forward and along the length of her and out the stern ports and doorway.

I always remember after awakening that I have dreamed the same dream many times, but in sleep it is always new. Back in that tumbledown shed on the hillside at night, in the stink of the leg wound that has gone bad, rifle braced on a broken crate, trying to push the illusions of the high fever out of my mind so that I wouldn't get the crazies and imagine they were coming up the slope toward me through the patterns of moonlight, and fire at hallucinations and thus give them the chance to find me and finish it, then wait there and also kill the girl when she came in the morning with the medicines. Then something touched my shoulder and I knew they had sneaked around behind me.

I went in an instant from the dream to the reality of the touch in the darkness of the lounge, made a hard spasmed leap from that prone position that took me over the back of the couch, with, in the moment of take-off, my right hand snatching the little airweight Bodyguard, hammerless .38 special. I rolled noisily to the wall, and where shadows were deepest, moved swiftly and silently to the light switch near the desk. I could see a shadow moving away from the couch. Squinting in advance to avoid the dazzle of the lights, I came up into a crouch and hit the switch.

Vangie had been backing away. She stared at me, mouth sagging, eyes squinched against the sudden glare, and stopped there looking at me and at the deadly muzzle of the little short-barreled handgun. I let the nerves and muscles go loose, slipped the weapon temporarily into the desk drawer.

"Salvage business!" she said in a thin enraged tone. "Salvage? For chrissake!"

I yawned. "I didn't mean to startle you. You startled

me. There are some people around who don't appreciate me at all."

She was naked, her hair tousled by sleep. She moved back toward the couch, shaking her head. Nipple areas exceptionally large, dark, almost a plum red, making the breasts themselves look smaller than they were. Weaving of flat muscles over the curve of hip. Deep and powerful slope of the belly down to a pubic thatch like a patch of gunmetal-colored smoke through which gleamed the pale plump weight of the pudendum framed between the round and solid pallor of the thighs.

She sat on the couch and said, "Geez, my knees are like water. Touch you to wake you up and you blow up like a rocket or something."

I leaned against the desk. "Did you have something on your mind?"

With the automatic exasperation of the person who has been startled she said, "What does it look like I had on my mind anyway? Maybe I came mousing in here in the dark so you could teach me chess, hah?"

She sighed and leaned back slightly, relaxing, sprawled and straddled, putting one hand behind her neck, elbow akimbo. Her body had too specific a look. It seemed too earthily illustrative of function, in the way that some of the larger flower blossoms have such a fleshy look of process one cannot see them from a purely aesthetic viewpoint.

I reached to the nearby chair, picked up my T-shirt and tossed it to her. She caught it and looked at me and said, "You're giving me some kind of a message?" She shrugged. "Well, it wasn't what anybody'd call a great start, buddy." She pulled it on over her head, hitched herself up to snug it under her seat. It came to mid-thigh. She patted her tumbled hair and crossed elegant legs. "What I had in mind, McGee, I couldn't get back to sleep once I woke up, and I had this lousy little impulse, maybe a way of saying hello, or saying thanks. Or a way to make it easier to get back to sleep. What you should know, I wasn't going to peddle it."

I sat astride the desk chair, forearm along the top of

the back, chin on my forearm. "I didn't think you were."

She scowled. "But it could get confusing, because I am going to try to hit you for a loan. And you maybe wouldn't understand it *would* be a loan, really and truly. Two hundred bucks?"

"Okay."

She gave me a little of the expression she had used when posing for Meyer and deepened her voice. "So there's two good reasons to say thanks, Trav."

"Saying it is enough, Vangie."

She studied me. "Listen, I *know* that there are a lot of guys who get chilled off if they know a girl's been a hooker. But I wasn't going to try to pay you back with some kind of faked-up trick, Trav, honest. I'd want to make out for real, and that's something I've never peddled except sometimes by accident practically. Maybe it wouldn't be the greatest blast in the world, but you won't forget it in a hurry, and you can believe it."

"Vangie, stop putting me on the spot, will you? You're all girl, and I'm not a prude, and I appreciate the gesture, but you are not in my debt and. . . ."

"And thanks but no thanks? Sure." She yawned. "No hard feelings, Trav. I guess all these things, they depend on what you're used to. For some little spook working behind a big desk the last twenty years, he'd think I was coming on with the greatest thing since the wheel, but I guess a man who looks like you and has a boat like this can score just about whenever and wherever he gets the wants." She got up, winked at me, sauntered over to the table and lighted a cigarette, shook the match out. "We're still friends, Mister. Maybe . . . I don't know . . . better friends this way. Funny to have a man friend. Men are either trade or they're in for a cut of the gross. You and Meyer. Funny, crazy bastards. I get the feeling . . . oh skip it."

"What feeling?"

She came closer, stood in front of my chair. "It's silly. A feeling that you two *like* me. I was in that big bed thinking about that. You know all the garbage about me I told you. And you're still *nice*." Abruptly her amber eyes filled with tears. Her mouth twisted and she turned and walked away, keeping her back to me.

In a harsh half-whisper she said, "What I've been mixed up in, it's a lot better all around if you weren't parked under that bridge. And if they find me again, maybe that isn't such a bad thing either. Awake in there I was thinking there's no way you can stop being what you are. There's no way to hide from what you know. And having anybody *like* me makes it tougher. Before I came creeping in here in the dark, I was getting screwy ideas, like paying off the world by going to work at a leper place if they still have them anymore these days. Miracle drugs, they probably got them all cured and it's too late."

I went to her and put my hand on her shoulder and turned her around. She kept her eyes downcast. "We like you even if you don't do dishes, Vangie. And we'd like to help you if we knew more about it."

For a little while I thought she would talk. She sighed and turned away. "Oh hell, Travis, it isn't so much finking out as keeping you guys from knowing how lousy I really am."

She braced up and assayed a crooked smile and said, "A year from now I'll have forgotten the whole thing. I've had good practice forgetting stuff. Say, you think I ought to pay a little call on Meyer?"

"I think it would work out just about the same way."

"So do I. Anyway, I think I can sleep now." With a swift and sisterly kiss on my cheek, she left the lounge. I turned the light out and settled down again, the weapon back under the pillow where it belonged. I'd felt no slightest itch of desire for her, and knew why. It had been a white lie. I *was* a prude, in my own fashion. I had been emotionally involved a few times with women with enough of a record of promiscuity to make me vaguely uneasy. It is difficult to put much value on something the lady has distributed all too generously. I have the feeling there is some mysterious quota, which varies with each woman. And whether she gives herself or sells herself, once she reaches her own number, once X pairs of hungry hands have been clamped tightly upon her rounded undersides, she suffers a sea change wherein her juices alter from honey to acid, her eyes change to glass, her heart becomes a stone, and her mouth a windy cave from whence, with each moisturous gasping, comes a tiny stink of death.

I could not want her on any terms. But I could like her. And wish her well.

FIVE

THE NEXT DAY, after beginning it with considerable good cheer, Vangie became more subdued and restless as we chugged north up the length of Biscayne Bay.

When she came up in midafternoon to sit beside me at the topside controls, I asked her if she had decided what she'd do.

"Get off this thing after dark, Trav. God, just one clown has to see me and happen to mention to the wrong party that he saw Vangie. Then they start looking. I don't know if I could sit still for it again. I think I used up any guts I had, and if they get me, I'd scream myself crazy. The smart thing to do is use the two hundred for a long bus ride, and go back to blonde, then work waitress or something until I find the right contacts so I can go back on the track. That's what I *should* do."

"But?"

"So there's something fishy about this salvage business, Trav. About you and this boat, and about that gun bit last night. And when you hauled me out of the ocean, you had no idea of calling the cops, and you kept your mouth shut. I don't know what you are. I know you're not cheap muscle. You could be legit, even. But you know your way around, and you seem cool and smart and foxy."

Meyer appeared and said, "Private discussion?"

"No, honey. Stick around. I'm about to proposition your buddy here. In my whole life I never saved a dime.

52

In the last two years I've stashed maybe thirty-two thousand in cash. It's what you could call dirty money maybe, but nobody can say I didn't earn every dime of it, and it's a very little bit of a cut of the whole take. I hid it in a pretty good place. I'll tell you this much. I was partnered with a fellow named Griff. He's as tough and quick and solid as you want to find. Right now he believes I'm gone for keeps. He knows I've been squirreling it away, but he doesn't know where or how much. I know for sure that by now he's probably cleaned out my place, my clothes and furs and jewelry and luggage and color TV and my darling little car, and he'll be cashing that stuff in as fast as he can. And I think he'll have just about torn my apartment to bits trying to find the money. But it's in a good place, really, and if my luck is any good, he hasn't found it. With that money I could *really* make a run for it, with a lot better chance of staying in the clear. But if Griff hasn't found it, he'll be keeping an eye on my place for somebody to come after it, because how could he know I hadn't told somebody? Anyway, I think I can get a guy to help me just enough so I can get in and out, a bartender I think I can trust, a fellow who's had the hots for me real bad for a long time. Anyway, at least I ought to be able to get close enough to find out if it's too risky for me to try."

"Then what?" I asked.

"Then I come back and hide on this boat and I tell you where it is and you go get it for me, Trav. And you keep a piece of it."

"You wondered if I was legitimate. To this extent, Vangie, that I couldn't go liberate money that belongs to somebody else and turn it over to you."

"Somebody else!" She pulled the dark glasses off and looked directly into my eyes. That dark amber was as merciless as the eyes of the big predator cats, and as empty, and as hungry. "Dead ones, Charlie," she said. "You want to rent an accountant and divide it up and go stuffing it into the graves? You want to worry yourself, think about all the dead ones to come. Me leaving isn't going to stop a thing. They break in another girl. Listen, it's a tiny piece of the whole deal, and it's *mine!*"

I glanced at Meyer and saw that it had shaken him as much or more than it had shaken me.

"Ten thousand for you," she said. "How about it?"

"The standard fee is half. If I recover it, which means if I even try. That's something we'll talk over when you come back."

"If I have to come back. If I can't get in and out with it alone. Half is one hell of a cut, McGee."

"And half of nothing is still nothing at all."

"My dear," Meyer said, "if things should go wrong for you, wouldn't you feel better if you had written it all out and put it in a sealed envelope and left it in my care?"

She reached and touched his cheek. "You are the nicest, Meyer. So nice you'd have to blow the whole bit, and it would mess up my girlfriends and keep the law looking for me forever. If I get my hands on that money, I want to stay dead, thank you."

"Knowing that your . . . friends are still murdering for profit?"

"People are dying all over the place for all kinds of reasons, Meyer, and if I'm out of this one, it couldn't bother me less."

Well after dark, wearing the black slacks, white blouse, dark glasses, a white kerchief around her hair, and carrying my two hundred in the pocket of the slacks, she went trotting down the stern gangplank, gave me a quick wave and went off into the night. Meyer had moved back aboard his own boat. I drifted after Vangie and memorized the plate of the cab she got into, went back and wrote it down, buttoned up the *Flush,* picked up Meyer and went off to eat Chinese. When we got back, we went below and he hunched over his little portable typewriter and composed a summary as follows:

For the past two years Miss Bellemer, a hardened prostitute twenty-six years of age, has been operating in this area with a group of accomplices in some manner more profitable and more dangerous than common prostitution. Three women were involved. It can be assumed the other two are of the same stamp as Miss Bellemer. She called one of them DeeDee Bea, spelling uncertain. There was a strong impression that the operating unit for each venture was a team of two, one woman and one man. For a time she worked with a man named Frankie. More recently her partner has been one Griff. No names of other associates are available as yet.

Logic tells us that the operation was some variation of a confidence game, its success dependent on the allure of the women in the ring. Miss Bellemer admitted in an indirect fashion she had felt sorry for one of the victims, had in fact warned him, even though she knew she was placing herself in grave danger thereby. Apparently, despite her warning, the victim was disposed of. Because Miss Bellemer was sentenced to death by her associates for this lapse, we can assume that the victims of their operations have been disposed of through murder.

There is a strong hint of some persons in a position of authority over these three operating units of one man and one woman each. For the time being, we shall assume there are two, both males, and that one of them was the driver of the car that took Miss Bellemer to the place where she was supposedly drowned.

A check of the cab company owning the vehicle in which Miss Bellemer left this area proved that she asked to be driven to Broward Beach. This matches the labels in the garments she was wearing when rescued from the water. We may assume that she and the man called Griff have been living in the same quarters or adjoining quarters in the Broward Beach area. She left with the hope of enlisting an unnamed bartender, very possibly also of that area, in recovering some $32,000, which she had saved out of her cut of the operation during the past two years. It is possible she intended to trick the bartender into luring Griff away from their quarters long enough for her to retrieve the money she had hidden away and make her escape undetected.

Observations and assumptions of possible pertinence:

1. Miss Bellemer exhibited certain histrionic talents which could presumably be useful in a confidence game.

-2. A series of multiple murders can be successful only if the victims have neither friends nor family anxious to conduct an intensive search.

3. This area is a place where lonely and well-to-do men in their middle years come to begin a new life.

4. In casual conversation with Meyer, Miss Bellemer displayed an intensive knowledge of the shopping conditions in the various islands of the Caribbean, from Curaçao to Grand Bahama, which might well have been acquired through frequent cruises, then abruptly changed the subject.

5. Disposal of bodies at sea would constitute no problem provided the passenger in question was not known to be missing, but this would seem a curious and difficult situation to arrange.

6. Callous as it may seem, it is not difficult to imagine several people of the same stamp as Miss Bellemer carrying out murder after murder, provided some way had been found to reduce the risk.

7. The operation is continuing and is sufficiently profitable to warrant the swift and merciless execution of anyone who might possibly endanger it.

8. As an estimate of the size of the operation, assuming Miss Bellemer's savings were fifty per cent of her percentage, and that she received twenty-five per cent of the take on each individual operation, we can extrapolate somewhere around $400,000 gross for the three couples during the two-year period. It is more likely she saved but twenty-five per cent, which would indicate a probable total gross of three quarters of a million dollars.

"Meyer," I said, "you have a curious mind."

"And," he said comfortably, "some excellent pictures of the bitch."

"And you forgot that she started to call the driver of that convertible something. Ma. . . . As in the beginning of Mack, Manny, Manuel and so forth."

"Forgot that. Another thing I meant to put in. She said she and Griff had to lie low when they got back from an operation. Makes the cruise more of a likely idea."

"And another item. A guess. They'll have to recruit and train a new girl to work with Griff."

We had gotten right up to the point of asking the question. It was almost a tangible thing, something that lay puddled on the cockpit deck between our chairs, steaming and stinking in the warm night. I had been saving my tobacco ration, my single evening pipe. I tugged the pouch out of the side pocket of my slacks, unzipped the pipe compartment, took out the Charatan sent me long ago by a lovely and grateful client with superb taste. The shape is Bell Dublin. It is a straight grain of Coronation quality. Before sending it to me from London she had some small silver numbers inlaid in the heavy part of the bit. 724. The twenty-fourth night of a memorable July, a little code which, if her husband Sir Thomas could interpret it, would bring him in search of McGee, complete with horse whip and incipient apoplexy. I packed it carefully with Erinmore Flake. Whenever, in the rotation of my small assortment, I work my way around to the Charatan, though it is an excellent pipe to smoke, I feel somewhat pretentious and effete. I can never completely overcome my middle-class reservations sufficiently to take a two-hundred-and-fifty-dollar pipe for granted. I keep kitchen matches and cleaners in the pipe compartment of the pouch. I lit it. The pulsing flame illuminated my face.

An angular girl-shape walking along the dock stopped and said, "Hey, Trav. Hey, Meyer."

"How you, Sandy?"

"Oh, just fine. Didn't know you got back."

"Tied up about dark. What's new?"

"Babs made it. Twins like the doc said it would be. Twin boys. Day before yesterday. And Barney was out on a half-day charter last week, Thursday I think, fifteen miles southeast, and a waterspout ran right over him, over the transom and off over the bow and swung around and nearly got him again. Didn't hurt anybody. Tore the outriggers off, turned his aerial into a pretzel, lifted up all the loose gear and took it away. You got to hear him tell about it, honest to God, it's the funniest thing I ever heard. I'm looking for Lew. You seen him?"

"No, we haven't."

"I was just checking to see if maybe he was having a drink with the Tiger. You see him, please tell him I'm home and that doctor phoned from Orlando and wants to start that three-day charter tomorrow noon, a party of three."

She walked away into the night. We heard discordances of music, night laughter, and somebody firing his fifty-six shooter on television. Meyer went below and returned with two cold brews, sat down with a heavy sigh and said, "What it is, of course, is a question of involvement."

"Keep talking. I know how I'm going to vote."

"I wrote that all out to organize it in my mind. She's not aware of how much she told us. Maybe it's enough, maybe not. That's more in your line. You'd know the next step. I don't. That is, if anybody takes that step. Question. Should a reasonable man, knowing what we know, and guessing what we have guessed, involve himself? Going down after the girl into that water was a clear-cut problem, and your response was instinctive. What we are talking about, I suppose, is the lives of a bunch of men we've never seen, men walking around. Thirty people watch a girl get knifed. A man lies dying of a coronary on a New York sidewalk, with the pedestrian traffic parting to move around him, like a stream moving around a boulder."

"And," I said, "you have this button and if you push it you get ten grand and ten thousand Chinamen die. And if a man is dumb enough to get himself mouse-trapped. . . ."

"And if a tree falls in the desert and there is nobody to hear it, does it actually make any sound?"

"Meyer, I've changed my mind. I was going to vote no. I am not going to vote yes. I am just going to think about that no until this time tomorrow. I have nice green stuff in my lockbox, enough so it will be next Christmas before I have to think of beginning to look around for somebody who needs somebody to handle a little problem. But."

"Yes indeed. But."

"Aren't you the one who says that's a dangerous word?"

He ignored the question. "Our Vangie, case-hardened though she is, got herself involved in something that dismayed her, and her revulsion built until she finally tried to pull down the whole structure. The impulse that made her do it was essentially suicidal. Consider her totally antisocial attitude prior to the past two years, Travis. To her mind, the world was corrupt and indifferent. As a child whore she knew the only imperative was to survive. She probably took some kind of hard pride in thinking herself capable of anything. She tried to tell herself that murder for profit was fine, if you could get away with it. But, over two years, actually being a part of such a thing eroded her false image of herself. And there, my friend, I think we have the reason for all the talk. Woman in search of herself. Trying to explain herself to herself—in front of witnesses. She had been a stoic about being dropped off the bridge because she had a guilt that required punishment. And even while she kept saying she wouldn't tell us anything about the past two years, the little bits kept coming into her monologues. Names. Terry, Griff, DeeDee. Hints and allusions. It was a two-day confessional, Travis. And. . . ."

I got up quickly. I forgot the lack of headroom aboard the *John Maynard Keynes*. I whammed my head into the overhead solidly enough to tip the world on edge and flood my eyes with tears. Meyer stared at me in astonishment.

When I could speak I said, "Leave us not have so much effing cerebration about the bitch. Okay?"

"What's been wrong with you these two days, Travis?"

"Wrong? How?"

"Sit down. You can't straighten up in here anyway. You haven't been the life of the party boat, boy. Rigid, tense, remote."

I sat, fingered the knot on the top of my head. "I ran a ten-day clinical service."

"It wasn't that, because you were peaking very nicely when I came down to fish. Now suddenly this explosion of irritation."

"I got tired of talking about the bitch."

I was glowering at him. Suddenly the Meyer smile began and widened. You can't stay irritated with Meyer. He nodded and chuckled.

"I should have figured it out sooner," he said.

"Tell me, O wise man."

"A dedicated archaeologist, at enormous risk to himself, descends into a cavern and comes up with a lovely figurine. He is an expert. He cherishes the form of ancient art. This one is rare and beautiful. His romantic heart bubbles over. Then he turns it over and looks at the base and there is the curious inscription: 'Made in Scranton, Pennsylvania.' So it has no value. Cheap goods. But it is so damnably lovely the poor archaeologist sits and looks at it and broods over what might have been."

"Very funny."

"And a little sad, boy. You like women as people. You do not think of them as objects placed here by a benign providence for your use and pleasure, so in that sense you are not a womanizer. But you cherish the meaningful romantic charade. Friend, you have been sulking. You have had your nose flattened against the candy store window, even though you knew all the candy in there was made of putty, and if you broke in and gobbled, it would make you deathly ill. Perhaps, five years ago, you would have made the ghastly mistake of trying to transform the bitch with the power of love, because she is decorative, spirited, shrewd in her fashion. You are wise enough to know she is case-hardened beyond redemption, but it has still made you wistful and sulky and depressed."

I pondered the diagnosis. Then I threw my head back and laughed at myself. Valiant knight trapped on a merry-go-round, scowling and trying for the brass ring with the tip of the rusty lance, knowing that if he got it, all he'd get would be another ride to noplace.

"Welcome back," Meyer said. "What's the program?"

"Wait and see if she comes back for help. If she does, we play it by ear, with the idea of conning her into giving us the whole package and letting us line up a lawyer who can drive a good bargain with the law so she takes the smallest beating possible. If she doesn't come back, then we go find the rest of the pieces ourselves and bust the operation wide open and let the law pick up the stragglers."

"We?"

"You're involved, Meyer. I can use that orderly brain."

"All my effing cerebration?"

"To balance the McGee habit of bulling my way in and breaking the dishes. And if we come out of it with a little meat, we share."

SIX

AT FIVE O'CLOCK the following evening, I waited on a bench in the hallway of the Broward Beach police station for ten minutes until a Detective-Sergeant Kibber, a knuckly middle-aged man with a tenant farmer face, wearing brown slacks and a shiny blue sports shirt hanging outside the slacks, came and sat down beside me and asked me my name, address and occupation. I showed him my Florida driver's license. In the blank for occupation is typed Salvage Consultant.

"Who do *you* think she is, Mr. McGee?"

"It's just a hunch. I had a date in Lauderdale last night with a girl named Marie Bowen. A first date. She didn't show. And . . . well, hell, Sergeant, I can't remember the last time anybody stood me up. I was going to meet her at a bar. She never showed up."

"Know her address?"

"I expected to find out what it was last night. We'd been in the same party one other time, and I remember her saying she had friends up here, or a family or something. So when the description of the hit and run, and how it was a girl maybe her age and hair color, came over the radio and it said you didn't have an identification, I thought I could . . . find out for sure."

"We still haven't made her, but we got the car about noon. Somebody stuck it in an empty lot, residential area. It was clouted off a shopping center lot sometime before eleven last night. The guy who owned it was in the movies there with his wife. This year's Olds. It figures to be kids. We're getting more of that than we should. It was wiped clean. The stupidest kid knows enough for that. When they clout a car it's a pack of them, and one will open up. A thing like this, a kid can't handle it too long."

He turned to an empty page in his pocket notebook, wrote, tore it out, handed it to me. "You take this over to City Memorial, give it to the fellow there that's on duty in the morgue. Six blocks west from here. If it's this Marie Bowen, you phone me from there, otherwise, thanks for the effort. And if it is or it isn't, it still won't be any fun taking a look."

I looked at the note on the way out. It gave me a strange jolt. "Give bearer a look at the Jane Doe. Kibber."

The Gray Lady at the visitor's desk directed me to the right corridor. The down stairway was at the end. Basements are a rarity in Florida. It was all linoleum and battleship gray. A colorless young man sat at a steel table under a hanging lamp reading a tattered *Playboy*. He took the note, crumpled it and dropped it into a wastebasket, got up and led me to a heavy door, pushed it open, turned on the inside lights. It was a small chilly room with lots of pipes and ducts suspended from the ceiling. They had a filing system I had never seen before. They were modular installations, looking like heavy office filing equipment. The doors were gray steel, about six and a half feet long, horizontal, and eighteen inches or so high. Each storage case was four bodies high. They had three of them. I saw that a small ruby light glowed on the edge of the case next to an off-on toggle switch on five of the drawers, the two middle ones in two of the four-high units, and one of the middle ones in the third. They were the ones at the handiest height.

He took hold of the handle on one of the doors, lifted it and slid it back into a slot above the body compartment. He pulled the shelf which held the body outward. It rolled easily on its bearings. It clicked to a stop at the limit of its transit, and a bright built-in lighting system came on automatically. All the light was focused on the cotton sheet covering the body. I felt against my face a stir of air colder than that in the small room.

He reached and took the sheet and slowly turned it down. He turned it all the way down to her waist, and moved just a little bit to the side.

I imagine they had left the eye open to aid identification. The other side of her head and the other side of her face could be identified as having probably been of human origin. From the waist down it was not a woman-shape under the sheet, just a lumpiness like a bed carelessly made up to resemble someone sleeping there, and the shoulder on the bad side of her was pushed in in a curious and sickening way.

I looked at that eye. An eye which has dried has an oddly dusty look. Like a cheap glass eye in a stuffed owl. It was the color I knew it would be. Darker than amber. With green flecks near the pupil.

I looked at the young man. He was standing there, staring at her breasts which he had so unnecessarily uncovered, his underlip hanging away from his teeth.

"You!"

He gave a little start. "Uh . . . can you give us an I.D.?"

"Sorry, no."

He covered her up. As he started the drawer back in, the lights went off. He pulled the door out and swung it down and clicked it in place. As we headed back out I said, "Why don't you go get yourself a live one?"

"Huh?" He turned the room light out, pulled the door shut. He rubbed his mouth with the back of his hand. "Sure, buddy, if I could find one of those. Even that messed up you can tell it was built like it wouldn't never quit. About the only thing didn't get mashed was the tits, but you can tell it had everything to go with them. A stack, buddy." He sat down, winked, picked up his *Playboy* and said, "See you around."

It had happened a few minutes after midnight on a downtown street. The proprietor of the corner magazine store was a real expert, the kind who raises his voice to let everybody within fifty feet enjoy the analysis.

"Nighttime, friend, this street is dead, everything closed, but you know this town, it's a real fast north-south street, hardly any lights, and all stop streets coming in. I opened up real early, and this morning before I opened up, friend, I went and took me a good look and figured it out. Now those kids were going like hell, no getting around that. So right in the middle of this block that woman, more than likely a little drunk, she comes tottering right out in front of them. At that speed, the kid driving didn't have a prayer of stopping. So what is the logical thing for him to do? What would you or I do, friend? What we would do is swerve toward the curb and cut around behind her. Right? So she sees those headlights coming like hell, and instead of keeping going, and she would have been okay if she had, she spins around and tries to get back where she came from. Pow! So he was going full speed, and where he caught her was about two feet from the curb, caught her with the right side of the front of that stolen car. There were still some little bits of glass sprinkled around there at the point of impact, and the places where the cops put sand or something on the blood. I paced it off, and that poor woman went thirty feet through the air, and they hosed it clean later, but this morning you could see where she hit the front of the Exchange Building just below a second story window, and she bounced off of the stone front, a glancing blow like, and she landed dead in the middle of the sidewalk another fifteen feet further on, so all told it was forty-five feet from where she got hit to where she came to rest, and friend, you can bet your bottom dollar that poor woman didn't feel a thing. Once you figure it out logical, you can see why there aren't any skid marks at all, and anybody in that car feeling the thud of how hard she got hit, they'd know there was no point in trying to find out how bad she was hurt. One time five or six years ago I was night driving over across the state, heading west about ten miles this side of Arcadia on State Road 70, straight as a string, no traffic, going about seventy, and a doe came running out of no place and I hit her dead square on, must have knocked her twenty feet into the air. Took out my headlights, smashed the grill and the radiator and buckled the hood up. I fought that car in the dark and got it stopped without rolling it, way off next to a range fence maybe fifty feet off the road, lucky to be alive. I tell you, that's a real sickening sound, that thud when you hit a living thing. But neither my doe or that woman knew what hit them."

I could imagine Vangie had known what was going to hit her. I could guess she might have even ridden in the car they killed her with. And she had stood there in the shadows, waiting for it to go around several blocks after they let her out, her and the man who stood behind her, big hands clamped on her elbows. Two or three blocks perhaps, to get up the speed to make it absolutely certain, then she'd see the headlights coming fast, maybe with some blinking to make identification certain, and then she'd feel the grasp tighten, and she would try to brace her feet, but the brutal shove would send her floundering out, while the man who held her dodged swiftly back to avoid being spattered, then walked swiftly to the corner, walked another half block, got into his own car and drove sedately away. I wondered if this time Vangie had broken, if she had begged and blubbered and wet her pants and had to be held upright to be shoved out into the path of the chromed juggernaut.

I had the strange conviction somebody was going to tell me all about it some day. Unwillingly.

So here we go again, noble brave name Key-Hoe-Tee? Wasn't the world maybe just a little bit better off minus one slut? Did it grab you that much, boy, to have that seasoned meat offered to you on a platter? Did it squinch your sentimental Irish heart to see the lassie roll her lonely hips in the solitary dance? How can you know the whole thing wasn't all lies, that she didn't try to cross up her fellow assassins and grab all the loot for herself and that's why she got dropped off a bridge? How do you know the whole scheme, whatever it is, isn't something she cooked up all by herself?

Maybe, for me, the only true knowing of her was down there in the black press of the outgoing tide, my fingers wrapped in her hair, feeling the frail questioning grasp of the girl-hands on my wrist, then feeling the girl-shapes of her as I pulled myself down her body to the wired ankles. All right. So that was it, the awareness of the life down there, going out of her quickly, the desperation and the stubborn wire and the haste. It was a difficult thing to do. You feel good to do a thing like that. And then when they take what you saved and see how high they can splash it against a stone building, you get annoyed.

Okay, hero. Tip the cops. It's their job.

But there is thirty-two thousand floating around somewhere. It needs a new home. And you've invested two hundred already.

It was quarter to ten that night before Meyer rang my bell and came aboard. He handed me a big manila envelope and said, "It took a goodly amount of sweet talk. Homer's wife expected to be taken to the movies. The last thing she wanted was some old camera club chum to show up with a problem. As a photographer, Homer is curiously limited. He takes macro-photographs of wild flowers of the southeast. He has thousands. But he has a very sure touch in that darkroom."

I pulled the pictures out. There was one big one, and I looked at that first. It was black and white, on semi-gloss paper without borders, a vertical shot, about eleven by fourteen, a closeup so extreme her features were larger than life size. It caught just the area from above her eyebrows to just below her chin, in quarter profile half turned toward the lens. You could not, of course, tell that she was dancing. She was looking down, the wing of dark hair nearest the lens swinging forward, covering part of her cheek. Her eyes were half closed. It had a luminous loveliness, the way the light lay across her face, the delicacy of it, a slight softness of focus, a look of dreaming. The angle somehow emphasized the oriental look of her. I looked at it a long time.

"This is a dandy, Meyer."

"Better than I could have hoped. That is about thirty percent of the frame. Sooner or later that one will win me a small piece of change. You might enjoy the title I've decided to give it. 'The Island Bride.' "

I thought of what a stone wall and a cement sidewalk had done to most of that face and put it aside and looked at the others. There were four enlargements, all five by seven, glossy, in sharp focus. They were the four shots he had taken when she had begun posing.

"Those seemed best for your purposes, Trav."

"They are. And the ones that will fit in my wallet?"

"In the glassine envelope there. Exactly the same four as the five-by-sevens."

"Got them. Good."

"Trav, don't you think I could be some kind of help in this. . . ."

"Maybe later. If I find more to go on. I'm going to find a place up there to hole up. When I'm ready for you, I'll call you."

"Don't . . . get careless."

"Nobody could get a good look at her and get careless." I saw that it was a few minutes past ten. I reached and switched the little Jap television to the unaffiliated channel that gives local news at that hour. A youth with many tricks with the eyebrows barked world affairs at us. He's the one that pronounces it Veet Nee-yam.

Soon he got around to our girl. "Earlier this evening the Broward Beach police made a positive identification of the mystery woman in last night's hit and run fatality. Word came back that her fingerprints are definitely those of Miss Evangeline Bellemer, age twenty-six or twenty-seven. The last address on file for her was a Jacksonville address. They do not know yet if she was living in this area. She had a record of several arrests for soliciting, public prostitution, indecent exposure, extortion and attempted extortion. Police are conducting an intensive hunt for the driver of the stolen car, and expect to make an arrest very soon, according to informed sources." I clicked the fellow off.

"From what she said," Meyer said, "I thought she was given better protection than that."

"Check it out and you'll find some convictions, but I doubt you'll find any time served. It's the standard deal, Meyer. The cops who are on the take have to bring a few of them in now and then, when they're sure of who'll be on the bench. The gals take turns, plead guilty, pay the fine and draw a suspended sentence. The law looks good, and from the viewpoint of the people operating the vice business, a girl who has a record is easier to keep in line."

"Sometimes, McGee, you make me feel naïve."

"Stay as sweet as you are. Time for one game?"

"If you promise if you get white not to open with that infuriating queen's gambit."

South of the city of Broward Beach, along A1A, is where the action is. The junk motels, bristling with neon, squat on the littered sand, spaced along the beach areas, interspersed with package stores, cocktail lounges, juice stands, auction parlors, laundromats, hair stylists, pizza drive-ins, discount houses, shell factories, real estate offices, tackle stores, sundries stores, little twenty-four-hour supermarkets, bowling alleys and faith-healers. The sprawl continues down through the continuous satellite communities of Silvermoor, Quendon Beach, Faraway and Calypso Bay.

I had left my venerable Rolls-Royce tethered in her stall. It was no occasion for anything as conspicuous as the electric blue of old Miss Agnes, who, during her darkest hour, had been converted by some maniac into a pickup truck. I cruised in my inconspicuous rental Ford and decided upon a motel called the Bimini Plaza. I did not know if it was in Silvermoor or Quendon Beach, nor could I think of any reason why I should care. It merely looked a little richer than the others, and had, according to its sign, three pools, three bars and inimitable food. It also had a bad case of vacancy, a

June problem that usually mends itself in July. I took their best, a large room at the ocean end of one of the three parallel wings. I had a salt-crusted picture window facing seaward, and a cleaner one facing the pool area in the inner court. I had two double beds, two weights of traverse draperies, a glassed shower stall, a large tub, a bidet, an icecube maker, polar airconditioning, remote controls for the color television set, and an ankle-deep lavender rug. For nine bucks, single.

The place was abundantly mirrored. There was a long one over the multi-level countertop which extended the length of the bedroom wall opposite the double beds, and one set into each of the sliding doors of the clothes closet, and one set into each side of the bathroom door. The bathroom wall above its counter top was all mirror, as was a smaller wall area in the bedroom, in the alcove where the dressing table stood.

In resort architecture this technique, which might be called Early Hefner, or Bunny Quatorze, is supposed to attract the wingers and swingers, the ones who beef up the bar gross, and who presumably have the disease of Narcissus to such an extent they get half their boots out of watching themselves *in flagrante*. The flaw is the concept that all the transient trade will be pretty people. Absolutely no ma and pa business of the kind where the total combined weight they could well afford to lose would add up to about the total weight of one of the svelte little lollipops the mirror-hangers had in mind.

As I walked back and forth, stowing the necessaries I had brought along, I kept seeing unexpected reflections of myself out of the corner of my eye, a brown slab of meat piled higher than is customary, the stride a loose-jointed shamble—knuckly scarified McGee-san, hoping that all dragons which need slaying will be the size of cocker spaniels, with their teeth and claws worn down from chawing bolder knights, their fiery halitosis fresh out of flints and fluid. In the silence of the room, in the manufactured coolness, mirrors populated the space with too many McGees, and I tried to dredge up a buried memory, and finally brought it into the light. Six days and six nights in a suite in Las Vegas as abundantly mirrored as this one, with that overly emotional heiress who had made the ghastly mistake of not only marrying a Seattle cop but giving him a power of attorney. The power of attorney was due to expire in six days, and he had laid out a very substantial sum to have her killed before the six days were up.

When we first holed up there, we had been almost right for each other, both in and out of bed. But the mirrors and the enforced togetherness kept pushing us further and further apart. She thought that all her tragic and humorless tantrums were a sign of emotional depths beyond my ability to comprehend. My gallows humor offended her. She felt any humor, any light touch, any mild clowning an offensive indication of the trivial mind. Toward the end, the mirrors somehow turned us into a lonely crowd, a platoon of tragic Arabelles and a squad of smirking McGees, crossing and crisscrossing the multiple mirrored images of each other like a flock of strangers roaming around a bus station. After the bounty on her pretty head ran out, and she paid me off, it was an indication of how enforced intimacy can cool things off to have her, at the airport, give me the same finishing-school handshake and remote glance and fleeting smile she would give an acquaintance whose name she could not quite remember.

I registered my appreciation of Vangie's playmates by deciding to carry the airweight Bodyguard at all times. It goes into the side pocket of the pants, the right-hand pocket. The spring-pop holster is fastened into the pocket. It was made to my order by a talented Cuban. Slide the open hand into the pocket, press just so, and the gun jumps solidly into the hand. It makes no bulge. There is nothing to catch on the fabric. Florida has handgun rules as curious as anywhere else. I own one acre of scrub land in one of the pork chop counties in north central Florida. Taxes come to $4.11 a year. The obliging sheriff renews my permit every three years. In Florida you can keep a gun in your car, your home or on your boat with no permit. You can carry it on your person on your own land with no permit. In certain areas you can carry it anywhere if it is openly and prominently displayed. But they do not like it tucked out of sight.

I can never tote it around, aware of the meager weight of it against my right thigh, without feeling a little twinge of theatrical jackassery. Carrying a gun, especially a very utilitarian one, has the bully boy flavor of the ersatz male, the fellow with such a hollow sense of inadequacy he has to bolster his sexual ego with a more specific symbol of gonadal prowess. Except for those whose job it is to kill folks, having to use a gun is the end product of stupid procedure. It is a handy way of correcting mistakes, so the only time to carry it is when you head into an area where a lack of information compounds the possibility of the inadvertent mistake.

I put the five-by-seven shots of Vangie under the patterned paper lining the shallow desk drawer. The wallet-sized shots were in the wallet. I had used the sample of her handwriting from her score-keeping chore during a three-way gin game, and had written across the most blatantly invitational of the four poses—"All my love from your Vangie." Green ink. Childlike backhand. Circle instead of a dot over the i in Vangie.

Time to begin. I looked out my side windows at the pool. Five little kids sploshing around in the roped-off shallows. I could not hear their shouts. I could not hear the shrillness of one of the red-brown young mothers who stood on the pool apron, shiny with sun oil, bulging her semi-bikini, her face twisted to ugliness as she yelled threats at the kids. The other young mother was supine on a sun pad.

The strange fragments of reality make patterns in your head sometimes. They form a collage that is static for a few moments, giving you the feeling that you are on the edge of some perception that might make all the rest of it a little more meaningful. The elements of this design were Vangie's dry amber eye, the yelping children at play, the barely perceptible weight of the gun, the slack underlip of the morgue attendant, and the adornment of the thickening body of the young vacationing matron in such a brief snugness of fabric that there would almost inevitably be another towhead added to her brood.

Very probably all perceptions are second hand.

The titled lady who had gifted me with the very expensive pipe had gifted me with something else also. When she insisted I read the poetry of W. H. Auden, I thought she was out of her mind. When I finally humored her, I found that it was not anything like what I had expected. And now this composite scene brought up from memory one of Auden's irreverent perceptions:

> As the poets have mournfully sung,
> Death takes the innocent young,
> The rolling-in-money,
> The screamingly-funny,
> And those who are very well hung.

SEVEN

I FOUND The Doll House on Sea Crescent Circle in Broward Beach. It was in a rich row of expensive shops. I parked on the circle and walked into the shop. It was cool, hushed, shadowy, smelling of fabrics and scents. Prism spots highlighted the display areas. As I walked in I broke the beam of an electric eye. A bell bonged somewhere. A girl came walking out of the shadows at the rear of the place, through the patterns of light.

She was dark, slender and pretty, and the front of her dark blue maternity smock was unmistakably bulged.

It was not yet noon. "Good morning, sir. May I help you?"

I knew that her quick glance had appraised the clothes I had selected to give the specific impression I sought to convey—casual and confident money, the kind that arrives on its own ketch or motor sailer. Boat shoes, khaki slacks, a dark green silk sports shirt, a very small edge of pale yellow ascot showing at the throat, a white denim jacket with wooden buttons, over the arm. I am considerably more plausible as a construction worker or a linebacker, but I have, over the years, developed the talent shared by bit-part actors and con men of giving a reasonable imitation of whoever is supposed to be wearing the garments. What I was wearing required amiable evasions, social pleasantries, and the air of being able to buy that part of town if a group of devoted people in the background recommended it.

I smiled into her eyes and said, "Nice. Very nice. The Doll House complete with doll."

The twinkle took precedence over the attentive politeness. "In the seventh month, that's good for the morale."

"Should you be working? Or are you the owner?"

"I'm hired help. The owner is Miss Gates. And it's good for me to keep working, thank you. This one is the sixth."

"And the little note of pride is well earned. I figured you for a child bride."

"I'll treasure that too. You're improving my day. Are you looking for a gift?"

"No. As a matter of fact I've got a fairly strange problem. And maybe I'm wasting my time, but I have a little extra time."

"You're not alone."

"I've got the problem because I have a terrible memory for names. I tied up down at the city pier over a year ago. I had a friend who lived here then. He's moved away. He rounded up a batch of people and we had drinks aboard, and it turned into a long loud evening. There was one girl in the group I thought I'd like to see again some day. She had a date that night. But . . . you know how it goes, she found a chance to let me know she'd be happy to have me give her a ring next time through. She gave me a picture of herself. Some kind of publicity shot I guess. I threw it into a drawer aboard the boat. This morning it took me about a half hour to locate it. Her name is gone completely. I tried to think of some kind of a clue, and all I could remember was overhearing her talk to my date about her favorite place to buy clothes in Broward Beach. The Doll House. So I thought I'd take the outside chance. Maybe you people know her name."

I took out the small picture, one without inscription, and handed it to her, and followed her slowly as she took it over under one of the spot lights. She examined it, gave me a quick glance which could have been a disappointed reappraisal, and said, "She's not a charge customer. But she does come in quite often. Andra . . . Miss Gates always takes care of her."

"How do I find Miss Gates?"

"She's back in the office, sir. If you will wait a few moments I will get you the information."

The chill was obvious. She had withdrawn and slammed the gates. I stood and stared into the glossy stylized face of a plastic mannequin. She stood on a round pedestal that lifted her almost up to eye level with me. She held her arms and hands in a position which looked as if somebody had just snatched her banjo away, and she hadn't had time to react. She wore a brief little shift in a coarse blue weave with a huge brass zipper from throat to hem, a little brass padlock fastening the zipper at the neckline, and, pinned to the bosom, a little spring-tension reel with the padlock key snugged up against it. An overhead spot shone on her straight, thick, cream-colored Dynel hair.

"Sweetie," I said to her, "your message gets through. May one day a plastic chap unreel your little key and tousle your plastic locks."

I felt fairly confident of the degree of risk I was taking. Vangie had spoken of her darling little car, of having a place to live. And if she had a record, and if it was a dangerous and conspiratorial game she was playing, it had to be under a different name. Otherwise the police would have had the local address very quickly.

Little Mother came silently back across the carpeting, handed me the picture and an unlined file card. I had heard a distant clicking of a typewriter. On the card was written Miss Tami Western, 8000 Cove Lane—Apartment 7B, Quendon Beach.

"Sorry to take so long, sir. As Miss Western pays cash, Miss Gates had to look through the delivery file. Some things which had to be altered were delivered. It would be three miles or so south of the city line."

"Thank you very much."

"We're glad we could be of service, sir."

I started toward the door and turned back. "None of my business, but there I was improving your day, and all of a sudden I'm Typhoid Mary. Would it help anything if I bought something?"

"I would be happy to wait on you, sir."

"Come out, come out, wherever you are, and tell me, please, why that picture turned you off?"

"I'm sure I don't know what you. . . ." She stopped abruptly, made a wry face. "Maybe you're not having me on after all, Mr. . . ."

"McGee. Travis McGee."

"Mrs. Wooster. Corrine. You give the impression of being able to find your way around, Mr. McGee. And if you'd never seen her in your life, that picture should give you some kind of a message. But you spent an evening with her. I don't want to say anything more. I don't want to knock a steady customer."

"I was under the spell of black velvets. From two o'clock on. Half and half, stout and champagne. They came aboard at six. If you've ever tried that magic potion. . . ."

She laughed. "Sure have. Everything gets such a *lovely* glow."

"That's why her name is gone too. And what she does. Some kind of an entertainer, I think. I mean that's the way the picture looks."

"Mr. McGee, you are backing me into a corner. I don't want to make any moral judgments. She has a lovely face and a lovely body. And we can guarantee she's well dressed. But do one little thing. Take a look at that picture again, and let's just say she doesn't sing and she doesn't dance, and she isn't an actress, nor does she entertain with *Aloha* and other requests on her musical saw. And let's say she distributes quite a few of those pictures."

I looked at it again. "Mrs. Wooster, you may have saved me from a very awkward little situation."

She lowered her voice. "If there was a chance of my being wrong, one small chance, I would have kept my mouth shut, believe me. But about five months ago she was here one afternoon with a little redheaded girlfriend, and it had been a long and liquid lunch. The girlfriend was DeeDee or BeeBee or something. They were both back in the fitting room, and there was a good customer there, too, and the customer said something which annoyed the redhead. I would guess that . . . the redhead actually has a better background than Miss Western. But, to shock the other woman, the redhead, who'd been sitting waiting for Miss Western to get her suit fitted, she jumped up and . . . like a circus barker or something, she pretended to be auctioning off the merchandise, patting Miss Western and turning her around and . . . displaying her charms and . . . saying what it would cost for this and for that . . . a kind of obscenity I never heard before. Miss Western was helpless with laughter. The other customer fled in tears. And . . . they weren't kidding. It was as if, all of a sudden, they had both changed into something we never saw around here before. They were both hooting with laughter when they left. And when Miss Western came in the next time, Miss Gates asked her not to bring her friend back here, ever. She took it all right. You just don't look as if . . . that is the sort of girl you'd want to look up. Or, excuse me, *have* to look up."

"Now you're making *my* day. But what sent the woman out in tears? Bad language?"

"The redhead was making some ugly comparisons. Andra visited her and apologized and said the redhead would never be permitted inside the shop again. But she never has come back."

"I guess this makes you the only friend I have left in town," I told her.

She sighed. "You know, it's a shame. I have a perfectly great gal in mind. So she's visiting her sister in Chicago. If I were you . . . I mean, trying to think like a guy, spending just a few days here, you probably belong to something that has some kind of reciprocal deal with the Yacht Club. They've got a pool and tennis courts and so on, and it's relaxed and friendly. What I *wouldn't* do is go pub-crawling down Sand Alley. That's the strip down the beaches. It is sort of what they call a little bit wide open. Let's just say there's a lot of different kinds of Tami Westerns, and people have gotten served some pretty strange drinks."

Off to the right of A1A as you head south are the random, unzoned living areas. Barren trailer parks making a huge hot aluminum glitter in the sunshine. Other trailer parks with shade and space and waterfront. Tract houses in clusters that vaguely resemble a game of Monopoly. Improbable groups of high-rise apartments. Curiously architectured conglomerations of condominium apartments.

I found Cove Lane a mile south of the Bimini Plaza, turning off A1A between a shopping plaza and a self-service car wash. Two blocks west it changed from business to residential. Number 8000 took up half of the fourth block, and was far more attractive than I had any reason to expect. They were garden apartments, single story, in gray weathered cypress trimmed with white. Ten numbered units, each containing four apartments—A, B, C and D—but so laid out, like the spokes of a wheel, with plantings, high basketweave fencing, access drives of white crushed shell, that each seemed to have a look of restful seclusion and the look of being near the sea.

A small sign advised me to inquire at Howard Realty, three blocks east, for rental information. There were little hooks on the sign, on which was hung a gray and white sign saying Apartment for Rent.

At Howard Realty, a sallow, spidery young woman with very thick glasses, a bright yellow blouse and bright pink shorts was minding the store.

"Eight thousand," she said, "is as nice as anything you can find up or down this whole beach. It shows what a real smart architect can do. But before we waste any time, Mr. . . ."

"McGee."

"The minimum lease period is three months. We've got five empties right now which you can believe me when I say it's unusual. And the summer rates right now on the cheapest are ninety-five a month without utilities, and that goes up to a hundred and thirty-five on the cheapest from November first to May first. Still curious?"

"So far."

"No kids and no pets. There'd be two of you?"

"Just me."

She took me over to an attractive wall panel, about eight feet long and three feet wide, in effect a map of Eight Thousand Cove Lane, with the road, drives, fenced patios shown. Pieces of plywood had been cut to the shapes of the ten structures and affixed to the panel and painted white. Keys hung from hooks in the plywood, under the number for each apartment. Five red tags were hung with five of the forty keys.

On a low table under the panel was a three-dimensional cutaway of one of the four unit structures, complete with furniture, little people, and toy sports cars in the carports.

"In half of them the layout is reversed," she said. "They alternate. But this is the way they're set up. In each unit, D is a studio apartment with Bahama beds. C is the small one-bedroom, like this one. B is the larger one-bedroom. A is the two-bedroom job. Heat pumps, wall ovens, tubs and showers, wall-to-wall carpeting, fiberglass draperies, private patios with redwood lawn furniture, completely furnished. We have, let me see, one A, two B's and two D's. So I'm wasting my time if I quote a C rate. The D's are ninety-five until November first, and the B's are a hundred and sixty-two fifty. Two twenty during the season. Being alone you wouldn't want that A, I guess. Two months in advance."

"How about maid service?"

"That's something you'd have to arrange yourself. We'd help you as much as we can, of course."

"I'd like to go take a look at one of the B units."

"If . . . you could come back about four o'clock. I'll be all alone here until . . ."

"I'm not planning to steal the lamps or the silver or the TV set," I said, taking my wallet out.

"I know that, Mr. McGee. It's just that. . . ."

I gave her four fifty-dollar bills. "Why don't you just

hang onto this for a little while, and if it's as good as it sounds, I'll be back and give you the rest of the two months in advance. Okay?"

Eyes distorted to hugeness by the heavy lenses inspected me, and she nodded and said, "Here. Hang onto the money yourself. I think the B's in the odd-numbered units are more attractive somehow than in the even ones. Two B and Five B. Here's the key to Five, Mr. McGee."

She lifted it off the hook and handed it to me. "Hurry back," she said, smiling.

I bent over the model again and said, "Is this the same layout?"

"Yes. Just like this."

I stared, trying to think of something to ask, demanding that the fates send me a phone call. After a few moments, just when I would have had to turn and go, they relented and sent me a mailman. He trudged in and said, "Registered letter, Bitsy."

As she went over to sign for it, I straightened up, plucked the Seven B key off the board and hung the Five B key in its place and, as I passed them on my way to the door I said, "Thanks. Be back in a little while."

I turned into the shell drive. I parked by the fence gate to Seven B. I knew that any slightest furtiveness could be dangerous, and so I walked to the front door, put the key in the lock, opened the door, and decided it would be more natural to leave it a few inches ajar. I knew from the intensity of the heat in the small foyer that it was empty. It was indeed a most attractive place. And hot. Within minutes sweat was trickling into my eyes. It took not more than three or four minutes to make certain it had been picked clean. No furs, no jewelry except costume jewelry. Plenty of underthings and resort wear and some cocktail dresses. Dressing table and bathroom countertop and medicine cabinet stocked with enough stuff to start a drugstore with a cosmetics department. No luggage at all on the high shelf in the closet. But about forty pairs of shoes. No sign of any personal papers or records or photographs. Big high fidelity combination with a stereo record player and a bin stuffed full of Vangie's kind of music. It was very neat and clean, the bed made fresh, turned down, clean towels on the towel bars. But there was the beginning of a little film of dust on the wooden surfaces. From the kitchen window I could see that the carport was empty. I found specific evidence in the living room. I tilted an upholstered chair over and looked at the underside of it. The material covering the springs and webbing had been removed and stapled back on. The staples were shiny. And they rust quickly in the summer humidity.

Two choices—Griff had located the bundle she had squirreled away, or he had satisfied himself it wasn't in the apartment. Or, a third choice, somebody had made her very very anxious to explain exactly where she had hidden it. A woman named Bellemer had died, quite badly. Another woman named Tami Western had gone on a trip. Car and luggage gone. When the rent ran out, the management would pack the rest of her stuff and store it, and when the storage charges were up to the estimated value, it would be sold off for the storage. No new problem when a girl's money stops. They pack the good stuff and leave.

Another few minutes and I would look as if I'd been standing in a shower with my clothes on. Just as I reached the foyer the door was pushed open. He was a broad one. Thirty, maybe. Orange swim trunks the size of a jock strap. Legs like a fullback. Flyboy sun glasses. White towel hanging around his neck. Black curly hair on top of a broad hard-looking head, and no evident hair anywhere else except some pale fuzz against deep tan from the knees down. There was too much belly, but it was such a deep brown he was managing a precarious hold on the beach boy image. He had a shovel jaw and a curiously prim little mouth.

"What the hell is going on?"

"That's a good question, friend. You'd think the way this operation looks they'd be smart enough not to try to rent one of these until they got the last tenant's crud out of it. Let me out of this sweat box, please."

He backed away and I pulled the door shut, tried it to be certain it had locked.

"You lost me someplace on this rental play, buds. There is a chick has it and she's on a trip."

I frowned at the key, showed it to him. "Seven B. The girl in the Howard office gave it to me. First, I tried to open five B with it. I thought that was what she said. Then I looked at the tag and tried this one."

"So it's just the key that's wrong. I saw the car. The door is open. So somebody could be cleaning it to the walls. They get some action like that around here."

A sun-drowsy girl-voice drifted over the wall from the adjoining walled court. "Who you talkina, Griff? Whozat, baby?"

"Just a guy looking, buds. They screwed up and give him the key to Tami's place, I told him she's away only. Mack showed yet?"

"No, and he din even call. How about that?"

"Well," I said, "thanks for straightening me out. Would you . . . recommend it as a place to live?"

When he shrugged those shoulders he was hoisting considerable poundage of meat. "Depends on what the play is. You got it private. Nobody bothers anybody. No kids mousing around. You got the big beach a quarter mile south, and even slow like now there's action if you want to check it out. For a guy single, you can't whip it."

"You work around here?"

"See you here and there, buds," he said and trudged toward the gate to the next patio where the girl-voice had come from. He wiped his face on the towel and went in and pulled the gate shut without a backward glance. I drove back to the office.

"They're really nice, aren't they?" said Bitsy.

"Furnished just a little more completely than I expected," I said and held the key up so she could read the tag.

"But . . . but . . . oh my God, did you walk in on somebody? Who's in that one?" She ran a thumbnail down a cardex list. "Miss Western. But I *told* you Five B!"

"That's where I went. The key wouldn't open the door.

I looked at the tag and saw it was for Seven B, so I thought you made a mistake about which place was empty. Don't worry. She wasn't there. A fellow named Griff, who seems to live in Seven C, saw my car and the open door and he straightened me out."

"She does go away quite often on trips." She spoke over her shoulder as she headed to the wall panel. She took the key from the Seven B hook and said, "*This* is the one I meant to give you. Darn it! It must be that maybe when Fred was sweeping up he knocked them off with the broom handle or something and put them back wrong." She stood there checking the other tags. "I guess the rest are okay. Do you want to look at Five B now?"

"I guess not. It's the same layout as Miss Western's?"

"The color scheme will be different, of course."

"Has she lived there long?"

She looked at the card again. "Almost two years."

"Well, she certainly keeps it clean and tidy."

"You were asking about maid service. I see here that she has a maid who comes in. We have to keep a record, so we'll know who's been given permission to go into the units. Are you interested, Mr. McGee?"

"Very much. There's just one other place I want to check, mostly because I promised I would, but I think I'll settle for Five B."

"Then you ought to grab it now. Even this time of year they don't stay empty long."

"How long would fifty hold it, not returnable?"

"Let's say . . . since this is Thursday, until Saturday noon? Then if you take it, it applies to the rent. You would owe . . . an additional two eighty-four seventy-five, with the tax, and forty dollars deposit on the utilities. We handle getting them hooked up in your name. But you take care of the phone yourself."

"Can you give me the maid's name?"

"Of course. Here. I'll write the name and address on the back of your receipt."

"Fine."

"She's a colored girl. She works for some of our other people too."

After I started the car and put the airconditioning on high, both vents aimed at my face, before I drove away, I read the name of the maid. Mrs. Noreen Walker, 7930 Fiftieth Street, Arlentown. 881-6810. I tucked the slip in my wallet, and from a drugstore in the corner shopping plaza I tried the number.

"Noreen, she be back along six o'clock from the bus, she workin' today."

So I used my afternoon time in sorting out the bars and cocktail lounges. You can make a guess from the way they look on the outside, from the names they put on them, but you can't be certain. You have to go in. You don't have to drink. Certainly not in the ones you can check off at first glance. You just go look up an imaginary name in their phone book and walk back out. I had no interest in the folksy ones, the ones with the neighborhood flavor and neighborhood trade, cute signs about credit, bartender being a jolly uncle, general conversations including everyone at the bar, and generally a couple of massive women named Myrt or Sade or Pearl bulging over the edges of their bar stools, drinking draft beer and honking their social-hour laughter.

By five-thirty I had found four probables. They were all within two miles of Cove Lane. Lolly's Five O'Clock, The Ember Room, The Annex, and Ramon's.

They all had certain things in common. Carefully muted lighting, spotless glassware, premium brands in the bottle rack, uniform jackets on the bartenders, carpeting, no television, live cocktail piano, dim and intimate banquette corners, the flavor of profitable professional operation. And they had that other factor I was looking for. You feel it in the back of your neck. A sense of being appraised, added up, categorized. I had drinks in those four. Plymouth over ice. At Lolly's and The Ember Room, the shot was slightly stingy, the price high. Ramon's did a little better. At The Annex the fee was a dollar. The gin was poured freehand into a squat thick-based tumbler, a knock better than two ounces, I estimated. The cheese spread in a brown pot was sharp and good. Couples sat in shadowy corners, heads close together, and they were served by cocktail waitresses in white leotards and high-heeled white sandals. Two stools away two florid men in business suits were arguing intensely about one of the provisions of a Swiss corporate setup. A slender girl with a very deep tan and a cap of curls white as snow, and an evening gown with only a double thickness of gray netting over breasts as brown as her arms, noodled a little golden piano on a raised dais, under a small rose-colored spot in a corner beyond the bar, making mouths to match her music. The bartender at my end had the happy face of a young, well-fed weasel. I left him a dollar bonus for the single drink to keep my image green. The bar was attached to one of the glossier motels. I went through into the motel and made some casual conversation with a desk man with a faint smell of authority about him.

When I got around to my key questions, I learned that the management operated the dining room and the room-service liquor, but The Annex was on concession.

Suspicion confirmed. The Annex would have a few sidelines going for it. The casual customer gets a heavy knock, good service in elegant surroundings. The aim would be to make just the costs on that business. The profit would come out of the live ones—live, fat and unwary. Just keep careful watch, sort them out, steer them into whichever behind-the-scenes plucking machine matches their vulnerability. Broads or beach boys, dice or cards, all staged elsewhere. It was nicely named. This was The Annex. The action was in other rooms, other places. The same kind of shuffle is available everywhere, from Vegas to Chicago, Macao to Montevideo. Sometimes it's a little smoother than in other places. Electronic technology has improved the efficiency.

I had to find out if Noreen Walker could fill in any blanks.

EIGHT

ARLENTOWN was the dusky suburb of Broward Beach, west of the city. Fiftieth Street improved as I neared her block. The little frame rental cottages were more recently painted, the fences in repair, the yards free of old auto parts.

I parked in front of her place in the evening slant of sunshine, aware of eyes watching me from up and down the block. I got out and stood at the white gate, knowing there would be no need to push it open and walk to the porch. A heavy woman, very dark of skin, wearing a cotton print, plodded out onto the porch and said, "You about the phone again?"

"I want to talk to Noreen."

"She live here. She my middle daughter. What about?"

"About some work out at the beach."

"Sure then," she said. "Just come home. Changing her clothes." She went back in.

I went back to the car and sat behind the wheel, leaned and swung the passenger door open. Through the open door, in a few moments, I saw her come down the porch steps, push the gate open, come to the car, her head tilted in inquiry. She wore blue sandals, bermuda shorts, a pale blue knit sleeveless blouse with a turtleneck collar. She was a tall slender young woman, very long-legged and short-waisted. She was lighter than her mother, her skin the tone of an old penny. She had a slanted saucy Negroid face, the broad nostrils and heavy lips. Her eyes were set very wide, and were a pronounced almond shape, and very pretty. Her breasts poked sharply against the knit fabric.

"Askin' fo' me, mister?"

"I phoned earlier and somebody told me you'd be home around six."

"Wantin' maid work done at the beach?" She was bending, peering in at me, manifestly suspicious.

"Would you please get into the car and sit for a minute, Mrs. Walker?"

"No need, mister. I ain't got me no free day at all. Maybe I could get you somebody, you say who to phone up."

I took the keys out of the ignition and tossed them onto the seat, toward her. I said, "Mrs. Walker, you can hold the car keys in your hand and leave that door open."

"Don't want no maid work?"

"No."

"What is it you wantin'?"

I had the folded fifty-dollar bill in my shirt pocket, and I took it out and reached and stuck one corner of it under the car keys. She moved away and I suddenly realized she was going to the rear of the car to glance at the plates.

She came back, looked in at me. "What you 'spect to buy?"

"Some conversation."

"You tryin' set me up someways, somebody con you wrong. Could be some other gal. I never mess with no white stud, never been in law trouble. I'm a hard-working widow woman, and I got two baby boys in the house there, so best thing you be on your way."

I got out Vangie's picture, held it where she could see it.

"That there's Miz Western. I wuk for her a long time, there at that Cove Lane."

"You used to work for her. She's dead."

For the first time she looked directly into my eyes. Her mouth firmed up, and I saw a shrewd light of intelligence behind her eyes.

"Fuzz doan throw big money to nigger women, 'less it's

got a mark on it, you come back a-raidin', find it and take me into town sayin' it's stole, and get me sayin' things to frame up who you think done it."

"I'm not the law. I just want to know what you know about Tami Western. It might help me get a line on who did it. I want to know her habits. And the longer we keep talking, the more all your neighbors are going to wonder what's happening."

"Big friend of Miz Western maybe?" She had a bland and vacuous expression.

"She was a cheap, sloppy, greedy slut. Where can we talk?"

"Where you from, Mister?"

"Fort Lauderdale."

"Down there any chance you know any Sam B. K. Dickey?"

"I worked with him once. A mutual friend was in trouble."

"Likely he knowin' your name?"

"Travis McGee."

"Please, you wait a piece, mister."

It was a ten-minute wait. Some children came to stand and stare warily at me from a safe distance.

She came back out and leaned in the door as before. Her smile looked tired. "Just to be certain, Mr. McGee, I asked Mr. Sam to describe you. He was quite picturesque about it. But it fits. And he said I can trust you a hundred percent, which is something Mr. Sam would not say too often about our own people. It saved us a lot of time to have you know him. I hope you *do* understand that the standard disguise is . . . pretty imperative. If you could come back to this area at nine o'clock, I think that would be best. Four blocks straight you'll come to a traffic light. There's a drugstore on the far corner. Park just beyond the drugstore and blink your lights a couple of times."

When I returned to that corner it was five after nine. She opened the car door quickly and got in.

"Just drive around?" I asked.

"No. Go straight ahead and I'll tell you where to turn. It's a place we can talk."

It was a narrow driveway, a small back yard surrounded by a high thick hedge of punk trees. There was a small screened porch, lights on, comfortably furnished. I followed her to the porch. She had changed to a dark green jumper dress, worn with a white long-sleeved shirt, with a big loose white bow at the throat.

As I followed her onto the porch and we sat in two comfortable chairs on either side of a small lamp table, she said, "Friends of mine." She took a cigarette from her purse, lighted it. "Very conspiratorial, I know. But we're getting very used to that these days, Mr. McGee. Mr. Sam said I could trust you. I'm one of the regional directors of CORE. I'm a University of Michigan graduate. I taught school before I got married. He died of cancer two years ago and I came back here. Working as a maid gives me more freedom of action, less chance of being under continual observation. Racially I'm what you might call a militant optimist. I believe that the people of good will of both races *are* going to get it all worked out. Now you can stop wondering about me and my little act and tell me what you want to know. You gave . . . an accurate picture of Tami Western. If she didn't travel so often, I would have dropped her from my list. That woman could turn that apartment into a crawling slum in about twenty minutes flat. About all I can say for her is that she *was* generous. Extra money, clothes she was tired of, presents men gave her she had no use for. But in a strange way, she made me feel . . . crawly. No one could live in Arlentown without being pretty much aware of the facts of life. But whenever we were there alone when I was doing the housework, the times when she wasn't sleeping or fixing her face or taking one of her half-hour showers, she was always trying to convince me how much better off I'd be selling myself to white men. She said she could give me all the pointers I'd need, and introduce me to the right people, and I could clear three or four hundred a week with no trouble at all. I just had to keep telling her no God-fearing Baptist church lady could do like that without going to hell for sure. It really shocked me to hear you say she's dead."

"Murdered. How long did you work for her?"

"I think . . . fifteen months. Yes."

"And she went on trips how often?"

"On cruises. Cruise ships to the Caribbean. Anywhere from five days to fifteen days. She'd tell me when she was leaving and when she'd be back, so I could clean it after she left and show up again the day after she was due back. She'd leave from Port Everglades. And she'd bring back some little present for me, usually. Those ships, you know, go winter and summer, all year. I'd say she went off, oh, a dozen times while I worked for her."

"Was there any predictable pattern?"

"Sort of, I guess. When she'd get back she'd stay at the apartment there, not going out at all. Sleep until noon, play those records, watch the TV, and do those exercises of hers. One thing about that woman, Mr. Mc-Gee, she kept herself fit. She'd lie down on the floor and hook her feet under the edge of the couch and lace her fingers behind her neck and do situps, dozens of them, just as slowly as she could. Sometimes she'd try on everything she owned and leave it all stacked around for me to put away again. And there were two girl-friends she had. Sometimes when she was staying home neither of them would come around. Other times it would be one or the other, and a few times they'd both come by. They'd fool with each other's hair, fixing it in different ways. And they'd play gin rummy. gambling. You never heard such language."

"Do you know the names of the girlfriends?"

"DeeDee was one of them. Small and redheaded and a little bit heavy. Let me think, now. For fun sometimes they'd use her full name, to tease her. It was. . . . Delilah Delberta Barntree. Usually it was DeeDee or DeeDee Bea. She seemed more educated than the other two, but she had the dirtiest mouth. And she was the same age as Miss Western, in her middle to late twenties, I think. The third girl was younger, early twenties, and very slender. She's a natural blonde, with very thick and heavy hair, that creamy kind, and she wears it usually in some way that leaves her little face sort of peering out from under all that weight, a pretty little face with sharp features and black eyebrows and black lashes. Not naturally that way, just to make more of a contrast. I don't know her last name. They called her Del."

"What kind of a car did Tami Western own?"

"A red Mustang convertible with a white top."

"How long would she stay in the apartment after her cruises?"

"A week or so. Ten days. Then she would start going out. Usually then she did a lot of shopping. She'd be out a lot in the evenings. And then she'd start not coming home at all at night, three or four nights a week, and when she was home and I was there, sometimes there would be phone calls and she'd lie on her bed and make love talk into the phone, and wink at me and make a face if I walked by. Once she was crying and begging into the phone to somebody, but it didn't mean a thing. The wink and the face were the same. Then after a while she'd start packing to go on a cruise."

"Did men come to the apartment?"

"No. She had a thing about that. She said it was her place and out of bounds and it was going to stay out of bounds."

"The man in seven C knew her. Griff."

"Yes. I know. A big man with a mean look. I don't know what the relationship was. He'd call up and she'd go next door for a little while."

"What if you had to make a guess at the relationship?"

She frowned. She pressed a slim brown finger to the corner of her mouth. When she stepped out of her housemaid role she had that slightly forced elegance of the educated Negro woman, that continuing understated challenge to you to accept her on her terms or, by not doing so, betray the prejudice she expected you to have. I cannot blame them for a quality of humorlessness. They carry the dead weight of all their deprived peo-

ple, and though they know intellectually that the field
hand mentality is a product of environment, they have
an aesthetic reserve, which they will not admit to themselves, about the demanding of racial equality for those
with whom, except for the Struggle, they would not
willingly associate. They say Now, knowing that only fifteen percent of Negro America is responsible enough to
handle the realities of Now, and that, in the hard core
South, perhaps seventy percent of the whites are willing to accept the obligations of Now. But they are on the
move with nowhere to go but up, with the minority
percentage of the ignorant South running into the ma-
jority percentage of ignorant Negro America, in blood,
heartbreak, shame and confusion. I hoped that this
penny-colored dedicated pussycat wouldn't stick her
head under the wrong billy club, or get taken too
often to the back room for interrogation. If, even on
the word of one of their shrewdest lawyers, Sam Dickey,
she was willing to trust a white man, it meant she
had a vulnerable streak of softness in her, which could
guarantee martyrdom sooner or later.

My intolerance is strictly McGee-type. If there were
people around colored green or bright blue, I would
have a continual primitive awareness of the difference
between us, way down on that watchful animal level
which is a caveman heritage. But I would cherish the
ones who came through as solid folk, and avoid the
slobs and fools and bores as diligently as I avoid white
slobs and fools and bores.

"If I have to make a guess," she said, "from what I
overheard, those three were lining up men who'd take
them on trips. They were whores who kept it from looking like ordinary whoring, and they'd clip the men for
all the traffic would bear. So I guess they'd have to
have some kind of protection, some muscle they could
call on if the customer got ugly about it. It had to be
something like that, with that man Griff scaring them
off. And maybe he even helped find the customers in the
first place somehow."

"When they were talking together, did the names of other men come up?"

"The other two kidded Del about some man. Somebody named Terry. They'd kid her in a very rough way, and she'd get angry." She shook her head. "No other names I can remember."

"Do you know if she kept much cash on hand?"

"I know she paid cash for everything, even the rent. But that's all I know about that. Oh, wait a minute. One time, months ago, I finished up and it was time for her to pay me the twelve dollars. She just had some ones in her purse and she told me to wait. She took her purse into the little kitchen and closed the swinging door. She was in there a long time. Five minutes, maybe. Then she came out with the ten-dollar bill for me. I don't think she worried about me being honest, not after the time I took a pretty pleated blouse of hers home with me to wash and iron for her. It was Italian, hand made, and she'd bought it in Nassau. The minute I got it wet, I saw the shadow through the little pocket, and there were four hundred-dollar bills in there, folded into thirds and fastened with a paper clip. I dried the money out and took it back to her the next time, and she thought it was the funniest thing in the world. I told her we good church-going Baptist ladies, we don't hold none with stealin'. She made me take twenty dollars for bringing it back."

"Did she tell you this time she was leaving?"

"No. I had to go there last Monday, expecting her to be in bed when I unlocked the door and went in. But she'd packed up and left. I looked around and saw she'd taken all her best things and all her luggage, so I knew it would be a long trip. It was a mess there, believe me, things thrown all over, empty glasses, drawers all open. It looked as if she had to leave all of a sudden. So I straightened it all up, made the bed fresh, and decided she'd get in touch with me when she got back."

"Just one last thing, Mrs. Walker. Would you know

where she usually went when she went out in the evening?"

"Good places along the beach, I'd say. Before she gave up smoking, that's what the book matches would say. The Ember Room, and Ramon's and The Annex. Places like that. And when the other women were there, sometimes they'd talk about places like that, who they saw there, things like that."

"I certainly appreciate your help, more than I can say."

"I want to ask questions about what happened to her, and I have the feeling you don't want me to."

"I'll make a deal with you. When this is over, one day I'll look you up and tell you how and why it happened, because by then there couldn't be any danger to you in knowing."

She nodded. "And I haven't talked to you at all."

"Right."

We went out toward my car. She stopped and said, "I'll walk home from here, Mr. McGee."

"No trouble to drop you off, Noreen. They've kind of shorted the neighborhood on street lights."

She turned so that the porch lights shone on her face. Suddenly she grinned in a mischievous way, giving me a glimpse of the wry humor she kept so carefully hidden. She backed away a full step, crouched slightly, and with a little snap of her right wrist, a slender four-inch blade appeared. She held it with an ominous competence, palm upward, knife hilt butted into the heel of her hand, thumb holding it against the bunched fingers.

"Mess wid me, you studs, you no use to no gal henceforth. Back off outen my way."

"I'm suitably impressed."

She straightened, sighed, thumbed the blade shut, slipped the knife into the jumper pocket. She looked up at the stars, no expression on her face. "We housemaids have to keep in character. This is the ghetto. The laws don't work the way they work outside. We're the happy smiling darkies with a great natural sense of rhythm. You can't hurt us by hitting us on the head. We'd still be nice and quiet except the Communists started getting us all fussed up." She looked at me and I saw bitterness on her face. "In this state, my friend, a nigger convicted of killing a nigger gets an average three years. A nigger who rapes a nigger is seldom even tried, unless the girl happens to be twelve years old or less. Santa Claus and Jesus are white men, Mr. McGee, and the little girls' dolls and the little boys' toy soldiers have white faces. My boys are two and a half and four. What am I doing to their lives if I let them grow up here? We want out. In the end, it's that simple. We want out, where the law is, where you prosper or you fail according to your own merits as a person. Is that so damned much? I don't want white friends. I don't want to socialize. You know how white people look to me? The way albinos look to you. I hope never to find myself in a white man's bed. I don't want to integrate. I just don't want to feel segregated. We're after our share of the power structure of this civilization, Mr. McGee, because, when we get it, a crime will merit the same punishment whether the victim is black or white, and hoods will get the same share of municipal services, based on zoning, not color. And a good man will be thought a credit to the *human* race. Sorry. End of lecture. The housemaid has spoken."

"When I next see Sam, I'll tell him that his Noreen Walker is quite a gal. And thanks again."

When I got turned around and headed out of the driveway, I saw her way down the dark street, saw just the swing of the arms in the long sleeves of the white blouse under the jumper dress.

NINE

A VERY TALENTED old-time con man once coached me very carefully in the fine art of appearing to be very very drunk.

At midnight, after having changed to an executive-on-a-convention suit, I reappeared, stoned to the eyebrows, at the bar of The Annex. I walked with the controlled care of a man walking a twelve-inch beam forty stories above Park Avenue. I eased myself onto a bar stool in stately slow motion. As I stared straight ahead into the bottle racks, I saw, out of the corner of my eye, the contented weasel approaching to wipe the spotless bar top.

"Good *evening*, sir," he said with that small emphasis which was in tribute to the dollar tip way back during the cocktail hour. "Plymouth over ice?"

I swung my stare toward him, without haste, focused ten feet behind him, and then on him. I spoke with deliberation, spacing each word to give it an unmistakable clarity. "I have been in here before. You have a very good memory, my man. Plymouth will do nicely. Very nicely indeed. Yes. Thank you so much. Very nice place you have here."

"Thank *you*, sir."

When he had put the drink down, he hovered. I stared straight ahead until he began to turn away, and then said, "Tomorrow and tomorrow and tomorrow."

"Sir?"

"What is your name, my good fellow?"

"Albert, sir."

"Tomorrow and tomorrow and tomorrow. Words of one of the poets, Albert. I made a great deal of money this month. A vulgar quantity."

"Congratulations, sir."

"Thank you, Albert. You have understanding. It is a rare virtue. My tax attorneys have arranged that I keep a maximum amount of that sum. My associates are eaten by envy. My dear wife will smile upon me. Tomorrow and tomorrow and tomorrow, Albert. In one of those tomorrows, I shall pry loose another plum from the tree of life. But will it be meaningful? What is the symbolic value?"

"Well, money is money. I mean you can't buy happiness, sir, but it sure takes the sting out of being unhappy."

"Unhappy. I knew you had understanding. And bored, Albert. The days become the same." I turned on the stool and looked around at the lounge area. The brown-breasted piano player had changed to a blue gown with a V down to the navel, and evidently with some concealed device which kept it anchored just unboard of the nipple areas. When I swung back I swayed slightly, closed my eyes, opened them again, lifted my drink and looked at the cocktail napkin. "Yes. Of course. The Annex. I have been in a great many places this evening, Albert. I have talked with many many many people. Few of them had understanding. They cannot comprehend the tragic trauma of our times. Someone suggested I return here. I have forgotten who. Perhaps I was misled. A rather large fellow, as I remember. The evening blurs. That is what happens to evenings. They all blur, merge, become meaningless. Tomorrow and tomorrow and tomorrow. Albert, I know you have understanding. You have proven that. But do you have tolerance for the mistakes of others?"

"The way I see it, anybody can make a mistake, sir. Right?"

"You are also a philosopher. My mistake would be tactical, Albert. The large chap at an unremembered place implied . . . get that word, Albert . . . *implied* that here I might find an ear, a little pussycat ear into which I could tell my tale of sadness, my need of cheer. Man is a lonely animal, Albert. And every place is a lonely place. If I have asked for some service the house does not, could not, would not provide, I am truly sorry for having offended you. I beg your pardon most humbly, my dear fellow."

He set to work increasing the gleam of an already polished glass. "Well, sir, let me say this. You won't find a nicer place on the beach. Now suppose, just suppose some girl comes in here. Now understand, I don't mean any hooker. I mean an upper-grade girl, and she's restless, and maybe something has happened, boyfriend trouble, and she's hurting a little. You understand? So she's at my bar and she has one over the limit and maybe her judgment isn't too good and some bum starts moving in on her. What do I do? When I say bum, I mean maybe he's got a two-hundred-dollar suit, a billclip full of money, he's still a bum in my book. What I do, I chill the bum off her, and when I get a chance, I see that she gets to be with the kind of man anybody can see is a real gentleman—like yourself, sir. That way nobody gets hurt. Nobody has any regrets. Anytime you get two nice people together, it makes you feel good."

"Albert, you continue to amaze me."

"Freshen that drink up, sir?"

"Splendid idea. But to go back to the topic again, it would mean I would have to be on hand at precisely the right moment. And so our discussion is purely academic."

"Sir, in one way it is and in another way it isn't. It's really kind of a weird coincidence you came in here tonight again and we got into this kind of a talk. It's like fate or something. It so happens there is this girl works cocktail waitress here. She's really a great kid. Just great. And the trouble she's been having . . ."

I held up my hand to stop him. I closed my eyes, swayed slightly, holding on to the padded rail.

"You okay, sir?"

"I do not mean to spurn your suggestion, dear chap. I wished one moment to recollect a few names the large fellow mentioned. Doubtless they are dear friends of his and, if I have the right place, well known here. A Miss Tami Western, a Miss Barntree, or a Miss . . . the name escapes me. Del something. Slender."

Albert scuttled back into his weasel hole and slammed his little doors. He wanted some time to reappraise the situation, and so he excused himself and went down the bar and served the few other customers in his section.

When he came back he said, "None of those ladies has been in here tonight." There was finality in his tone.

"Albert, we seem to be losing our rapport. Have I done something wrong?"

"Wrong? Wrong? A customer asks about another customer, so I say whether they been in or not. Okay?"

My hand was on the bar, palm up. I pulled my thumb back enough to expose the corner number on the folded twenty.

"A fellow as deft, as kindly, as helpful as you, Albert, would know how to get in touch."

Strangely, he hesitated, and then the twenty disappeared so quickly I half expected to see a little puff of smoke. He gave a cautious glance down the bar, then leaned over it toward me. His personality suffered an abrupt change. "Friend, what you just bought for the twenty, maybe you won't like. But you are getting your money's worth. Advice, you bought. I don't know if you come in here with a case of the cutes, or if somebody steered you to a busted mouth for laughs. Either way it would be the same. There's muscle don't want you poking in that direction, not those broads, not Western and Barntree and Whitney. All I know about that operation, they got no room for what you got in mind. I'm doing you a favor. Forget it. For half a bill I set you up with a good clean hardworking kid. You want to get something you couldn't forget so quick, hang around until two o'clock, for two bills you get the piano player, if after she looks you over she says okay, which she probably would because she isn't booked and what she won't take is fat or old, some kind of a thing about that, and either kid it would be for the night. But you come in here and give me the names you give me, friend, it has to turn me off. You following me?"

"Tomorrow and tomorrow and tomorrow."

"Oh for chrissake!"

"In the vernacular, dear boy, my earlier acquaintance was having me on?"

"He was sending you to play in the traffic."

"This muscle you mentioned, is it that dangerous?"

"You better believe it. Those broads can put on the cool pretty good, but if somebody doesn't take a hint, then they get a real good hint, like a kneecap gets kicked loose out in the parking lot."

"But with no style, dear boy. Punks, no doubt."

He shook his head sadly. "You don't *want* to believe me, sir. This is no game. Take my word. I don't tell anybody about what you asked, I'm doing you a favor."

I manufactured a shudder and some difficulty in focusing on Albert. I put a five-dollar bill on the bar. "Suddenly, dear friend I find myself in dire need of an empty bed rather than diversion. I have foundered on the rocks. Plymouth rocks. I trust we may pursue these matters when I have a less overwhelming sense of unreality."

With an egg-sucking grin Albert said, "Tomorrow and tomorrow and tomorrow, sir?"

"Exactly. We have each made a new friend, and so the evening is not a total waste." I walked my twelve-inch beam on out the door.

Back in my hall of mirrors, spread eagled and supine on one of my two double beds under the cave-breath of the airconditioning, I fit together the pieces I had, and I thought of them in three colors—green for the facts, yellow for the reasonable guesses, red for the ones I had to reach for.

It puzzled me that to be totally stoned and heavily solvent did not make me attractive bait. Perhaps they could handle only so much bait at a time. If they hadn't replaced Vangie-Tami, the other two might be diligently busy at the moment. They might both be off on cruise ships. They might be lying low until they were certain their previous ventures had not created unwelcome heat and attention. Or they could be setting up new pigeons—provided the execution of Tami had not made the group decide to suspend operations until they were certain she had not left them a little posthumous gift of trouble.

One Mack had driven the car that had stopped on the bridge over our fishing hole. One Terry had dumped her over. And her reappearance when the bartender she spoke of had evidently betrayed her trust must have come as a sickening shock to those boys. I knew there was little logic in my absolute confidence that Vangie had not identified me as the rescuer, no matter what they might have done to her. She would have to give them a plausible story of rescue. Some fishermen under the bridge. And, having her return to get her money would be an indication she had not exposed the operation. Had they broken her to the point of making her tell the hiding place? I knew why I doubted it. In free fall to what she believed was her death, she had stifled the instinctive scream just to give Terry an awkward time. Knowing that the second attempt would kill her for sure, knowing that she couldn't buy a thing with the money she had squirreled away, it seemed consistent with some inner toughness of fiber for her to deny them the money.

I was dubious about the next step. The possibility of tracing Vangie's bartender friend seemed remote. The aging shovel-jawed beach boy, Griff, would get very edgy if he should come across me again. Vangie's five minutes in that kitchen intrigued me. It was a small kitchen. It wouldn't take long to find out if the money was still there, or if Griff's thorough search had found it.

Getting into seven B the second time would be more difficult. I could be certain of one thing. I was not dealing with a group of early risers. Sliding glass doors on aluminum tracks opened from the apartment living room onto the fenced patio area. They yield as if they were made to be opened with a tire iron.

It was five after two. I picked up the phone and left a call for quarter to five.

This time I had closed the outer gate. The inner latch on the sliding doors tore slowly under leverage, made a little clinking sound as it parted. In the dark apartment, I pulled the kitchen door shut behind me, clapped shut the aluminum venetian blinds, turned the lights on and went to work. The time it had taken Vangie to get the money meant a fairly intricate hiding place, something which had to be taken apart and replaced. Stove negative. Refrigerator negative. Wall oven negative. Dishwasher negative. Some of the nuts that fastened housings on were cross-threaded, indicating somebody had been there first, but there was no way of knowing if any of the places had turned up the jackpot. I stopped and leaned against the counter by the sink. I checked the disposal unit. Removing that housing would be no five-minute job, and it didn't look as if there could be any space available inside it anyway.

There was a kick stool beside the sink, the kind that rolls on concealed casters that retract when you step on it so that it stands firm. It was to give access to some of the cabinet shelves built too high to reach easily. No clue in any of them.

I looked at the ceiling fixtures. The one over the sink was a double circle of fluorescent tubing, the kind where the base fastens against the ceiling by means of a knurled center screw. I moved the kick stool over in front of the sink and turned off the lights, opened the blinds. The day was brightening rapidly and soon there would be the first horizontal rays of orange sunlight coming in from the Atlantic. Without any particular optimism, I undid the knurled screw. The base came down and hung by the wiring, a foot below the acoustic tile of the kitchen ceiling. The wires hung from the countersunk junction box. The base was round, perhaps sixteen inches in diameter. A crude rectangular hole had been cut into the tile beside the junction box. I reached up into the hole and over to the side, away from the junction box. The first packet I brought down was two inches thick, fastened with two red rubber bands. There was a fifty exposed on one side of it, a twenty on the other. The second packet was thinner, with a hundred on one side, a ten on the other. The third was the thickest of all, with twenties on either side. The last one was medium, exposing a ten and a fifty. I shoved them inside my shirt and rebuttoned it. I fitted the base back over the threaded fixture spindle, replaced the knurled screw, got down and rolled the kick stool away. Vangie had made a shrewd selection. The hiding place was obvious and unlikely.

With a satisfying weight and bulk inside my shirt and with tire iron in hand, I went out the way I had come in. Just as I touched the gate latch, I heard a single crunch of a step on the brown pebbles behind me, and as I tried to spin, hard metal hit me briskly and solidly over the right ear. It wasn't meant to knock me down. It was perfectly gauged to do exactly what it did. With the echoes of the first red and white explosion going off in my head, I staggered back against the gate. The tire iron clanked onto the pebbles. That kind of blow on the skull creates a wave of nausea in the back of the throat, clogging and receding, coming back in diminishing force several times as vision clears.

In the increasing light I saw that shovel-jaw looked better in his flyboy sun glasses. His eyes were small, inflamed perhaps by his days on the beach, and his lashes were stubby, sparse and pale. They had the look you see in elephant eyes, a dulled and tricky savagery. He stood at a professional distance and held one of the most reliable and deadly of handguns aimed casually at my chest, dead center, a heavy Luger. I could see how neatly he had taken me. He had been tucked behind the plantings just to the right of the gate, perfectly content to wait there, knowing it was the only way out.

He hooked a toe under the tire iron, flipped it far to the side. "You keep getting the wrong key, buds."

"You keep pretty good track of this place."

"I run the wire from a little Jap intercom through the

wall, set it on dictate at full volume, the other half of it next to my bed. I get a week off one of those little nine-volt batteries. You came through loud and clear. I was expecting somebody. Not you. Somebody I know better. Turn real slow. All the way around. That's nice. Hands flat against the gate. Keep them there. Walk your feet back toward me. A little more. Little more. Fine."

Even then he was careful. Long reach. Quick little taps with the fingertips. Fortunately he tapped the money bulge before he made any further investigation of the slight bulk in the right hand pocket of my slacks. And it is such an unlikely weapon carried in such an improbable place, it will even get past most hasty police searches.

"Now keep yourself braced just like that with your left arm, and reach down and unbutton the shirt and shake that stuff out of there, buds."

The four packets fell. He tapped the shirt again at the waistline to be certain. Then he had me shift several feet to the side, maintaining the same helpless posture. Out of the corner of my eye I saw him squat, gather up the packets, the gun now in his left hand. They went into the front of his shirt.

He straightened up. "Where the hell was it?"

"In the ceiling, up underneath the big light fixture over the sink."

"Fifty hours I spent in there. So the bitch told you."

"Or maybe I'm not as stupid as you are, Griff."

"I don't make that kind of mistake, like letting you get me sore. I take it very calm, buds. I don't care who you are. I don't have to know who you are, or who told you what. All I have to do is keep my mind on this play until it's over. What you do now is open the gate very slowly, and you open it wide. And you walk slowly down the drive the way you came, with me behind you. And then you go around your car and you get in on the passenger side, and very slowly you ease yourself over behind the wheel. Let's go. There's a busted door, a tire iron. I try to fire a warning shot and it gets you in the spine. It's no sweat to me to testify, buds. Remember that. I'm clean as Girl Scouts in the area."

Never get cute with the competent ones. Amateurs with guns in their hands are dangerous, but there is almost always a delay before they can bring themselves to actually fire at a human being. The competent ones are not hesitant.

When I was behind the wheel, he closed the door, hitched close to it, rested the Luger barrel on his left thigh, aimed at my middle, his thick finger on the trigger.

"Get your keys, buds, and start it up. Keep it at thirty-five. Go out to the highway and turn south."

I was one docile fellow. I wanted no lead tearing through the irreplaceable parts of wondrous, inimitable, precious me.

"How far?" I asked.

"Keep going."

After a mile or so I said, "Did they make Terry do it the second time too?"

"He was away. Shut up."

"You could be making a mistake, Griff."

"So when I find out, I'll cry a little."

The beach clutter thinned out. He told me to slow down. He had me pull over onto the right shoulder until the road was clear of the meager morning traffic in either direction. Then, at his direction, I drove diagonally across the highway, up a rutted sandy track and pulled around behind a huge billboard advertising that oceanfront piece, eleven hundred feet of Atlantic Beach, four hundred feet deep from highway to tide line, for sale or lease.

The orange-red rising sun was lifting out of the sea, the gap between it and the steel blue horizon widening. He made no mistakes getting me out of the car. We walked across sandy hummocks, past tall clumps of sea oats. We came to a swale between brown dunes which seemed to satisfy him.

"What you do now, buds, very slow, is you lie down right there flat on your back."

"Now wait a minute!"

"When you goof a play, the cost comes high. You

should know a thing like that. The little ball drops in the wrong hole. Stretch out, boy. They find the Luger in your hand. After I put one in the side of your head, I even let you fire one out to sea in case some clown takes a paraffin test. There's no history on the Luger, and I put no prints on the car. The surf noise like that, who hears two shots? Nobody sees us here. We're out of sight. I was sleeping in swim trunks. So I roll the loot in my clothes and walk all the way back down the beach. Maybe I find a pretty shell. Who knows? Just stretch out nice, buds."

"Can I have a cigarette?"

"Don't use them."

"I got my own. How about it?"

"Stop stalling and . . . okay, light one. It'll look like you thought it all over and decided to take the jump."

I slapped my shirt pocket, reached into the right hand pocket of my slacks. The spring release jacked the little Bodyguard into my hand, and I fired once, falling to the right, rolling hard, every nerve arched tight waiting for the slug. I ended up in a prone position, braced on my elbows, left hand clamping the gun wrist to steady it. He was down. I saw his right hand on a slope of sand, the fingers opening and closing. The Luger stood upright in the soft sand a foot from his hand, barrel sunk straight down. I walked to him on my knees, holding the gun on him. I circled him, picked up his weapon, tossed it a dozen feet behind me. The upper right side of his chest had a spreading red stain sopping the thin yellow fabric of the sports shirt. He coughed weakly and blood ran from the corner of his mouth down into the coarse sand.

The reddened eyes looked vaguely at me. "Tricky bastard," he said in a half whisper. "Should have known you were taking it too easy. My play would have been check you out better. Christ, everything feels as if it was going all loose inside me."

"Where's Terry?"

"Screw you, buds."

"You aren't hit as bad as you think, Griff. The sooner you answer, the sooner I go get an ambulance."

He turned his head, coughed a heavier gout of blood into the sand. He closed his eyes. "Ans Terry. Him and the Whitney bitch. Monica Day."

Abruptly he opened his eyes very wide, threw his head back and stared at the sky. His body arched twice, thudding down against the sand, and he kicked his heels against the sand, then slowly softened and dwindled into stillness. The slug had evidently severed one of the big arteries in the right lung. It hadn't taken long. I stood up slowly, slid the Bodyguard back into the spring catch. I looked around. I could hear traffic sounds merged with the wash of the surf. It numbs, always, even when you keep asking yourself what other choice you had. Somebody watched him pull himself up by the crib bars and stand cooing and drooling, and thought him a damned fine baby. Far down the beach I saw an early morning family moving slowly my way. Two large shapes, two tiny shapes covering more ground. I reached down, yanked the yellow shirt out of the waistband, recovered the four packets, buttoned them back inside my shirt. I thought of wrapping his hand around the Luger and putting a second slug into the same hole. But who shoots himself high in the right side of the chest?

I saw a piece of weathered board in the sea grass, a splintered piece of one-by-six a little over two feet long. I squatted near the deepest part of the swale and, working as hard and as fast as I could, using it as a crude shovel, I made him a hole as long and as wide as he was, and almost as deep as he was thick. I checked his pockets, found nothing, took another look at the beach and saw how much progress the family had made. I tugged the body down parallel with the trench, then rolled him one half turn to drop face down into it. Next I slid my board under the Luger and dropped it beside his ear and used the board to shove it down into the sand. Like a nightmare bulldozer I crawled around the area, shoving the board with two hands like a bulldozer blade, covering him over, borrowing from all sides of the swale to fill the pocket a good two feet deep above his thick dead brown neck, and at one point heard myself making a small foolish whimpering sound, shut my teeth hard and cut it off. I stood up again, sweaty and weak. The family was heading back from whence they came, back probably to a motel breakfast. The sand was too dry to take any identifiable imprint. A footstep left a shallow pocket of sliding sand. I scraped the coughed blood under. There was no sign of him. The wind might uncover him in a day. Or cover him ten feet deeper. I walked back to the car. I had to think out the normal automatic motions of walking, lift of the foot, bend of the knee, swing and placement of the foot, and the alternate procedure with the other leg.

I backed the car away from behind the billboard, got stuck for a heart-stopping moment, rocked it free and came out to find nothing on the road except two big trucks, both receding in opposite directions.

I unlocked my mirrored room and walked into it, realizing I had absolutely no memory of the drive back. I looked out my windows and knew it was full morning, and I knew that when Griff had eaten yesterday's three meals, he hadn't any idea they would be the last three. I wondered if the girl with the sun-sleepy whine of voice was nested in her sleep in seven C, her body resting from Griff's use of her, dent of his head in the neighbor pillow.

The records say that forty thousand men disappear every year in this country. A great many of them stay lost. People don't look very hard.

I could guess what the others would think. Griff had been teamed with Vangie-Tami. The execution could have made him uneasy. If he came across her money and left, he would be difficult to find. I put the chain on the room door. I locked myself in the bathroom, put her money on the countertop, and with the little kit from the side pocket of my suitcase, I cleaned out the short barrel of the Bodyguard, replaced the missing round, shoved it back into the clip against the spring pressure.

I removed the rubber bands, sorted the money by denomination and counted it twice. Her guess had been optimistic. Twenty-eight thousand, eight hundred and sixty. Taking mostly fifties, I put the eight hundred and sixty into my wallet. I banded the rest of it into one solid brick, wrapped it in a dirty shirt and stuffed it into the glove compartment and locked it.

I took a long, long shower. I stretched out on the bed. So go home, McGee. Why not? It's just another salvage operation, only this time you get to keep it all. The wench is dead. And these are rough folks. Right now the sun would be burning down on your open eyes, waiting there for somebody taking a short cut to the beach to come across the car and then the suicide. Scratch one Vangie and one Griff. They cancel out. So go home. There's enough in the kitty now to take you to a year from Christmas, and a very lush year at that.

Sure.

And spend the whole year wondering at what moment they were knocking off what new pigeon, now that they'd cleaned up the operation by disposing of the one weak link.

Monica Day.

Who the hell was she? And why did she sound familiar? Bit parts? Ans Terry. Anselm. Ansel. Known as one big powerful son of a bitch who could kill people with his hands.

So, very probably, could Griff.

And so had I. And it didn't feel any better than doing it with a gun. In fact, it felt a little worse.

TEN

AT A LITTLE past noon I was back aboard *The Busted Flush*. I leave the airconditioner set to cycle when the inside temperature gets past ninety.

I put the thermostat back down to seventy, then went through into the forward bilge with my brick of money. My safe is an aluminum box. A child could open it with a church key. But the child who could find it would frighten me.

Forward, on the port side, below the waterline, I have a section of fake hull. Drill a hole and the sea would come spurting through, and keep coming, because there is an open sea cock that keeps it filled with about sixty gallons. There is a little lever which closes the sea cock. The lever is carefully concealed. I close the sea cock. I press an area of the hull just so. Then I can get a blade under the other end and pry it open. It swings on concealed bronze hinges. Thirty gallons or so rush down into the bilge and the pump starts automatically. I reach into the gap and down between the double hull section, and pull the box free of the brackets that hold it. I shake the water from it. It has a good rubber gasket, a clamp fastening with good leverage. I open it, put the brick of currency inside, push it back down against its buoyancy, back into the brackets. I swing the heavy curve of wood back into place. I open the sea cock. I hear the faint garglings as it fills again, up even with the outside waterline. The fake hull in that area is always slightly damp. One small artistic leak that trickles about a meaningless cup of seawater a day. I have a second safe, a barrel job, hidden quite carefully. I keep a few good things in it. Not too much. Enough to keep disappointment from being too acute. A man who finds something does not keep on looking.

And so, on that Friday, I went right from Bahia Mar to Port Everglades to check on Monica Day. More properly, the *Monica D*. D for DeLorio Shipping Lines. Day as in the Italian pronunciation of the letter D. The home base of the company is in Naples. From November through June they operate two small single-stack, single-class cruise ships out of Port Everglades. On the drive down I had remembered why the name was familiar. The sister ship was the *Veronica D*.

When I went over the bridge I saw three vessels moored there. One was the *Veronica D*. No particular activity around her. I drove into the port area and parked the rental car by the big customs shed. There were a few people around and a mild and aimless air of activity. Cases of provisions were being taken off a truck and put on a conveyor belt that ran up to an open cargo hatch in the side of the hull where the hands were grabbing the cases and stowing them. A man stood with a clipboard, checking the items aboard. I found a gate ajar in the wire fence and walked with an air of purpose to the forward gangplank. An officer in white was at the top of it, just stepping aboard. I went on up. There was a smart young seaman on the side deck, and he watched me walk up the incline and stood at attention, blocking the way.

"Sir, is not permitted coming aboard now. Is later."

"I want to talk to the purser."

"Is ver' busy now, sir, for the sailing. Five o'clock sailing. Much work."

I found a five-dollar bill for him, shoved it into his tunic pocket. "Why don't I stand right here and you run and find him and tell him it's important?"

After a little hesitation, he hurried off. He was back in a very short time with a man who looked like a fifteenth-century bishop. He had a regal manner, a spotlessly crisp white shirt.

"May I be of some help, sir?"

I led him a dozen steps forward, out of earshot of the gangplank guard. "A question of identification, if you wouldn't mind."

I showed him two of the wallet-sized pictures of Vangie.

"Do I know her? Oh, yes, of course. It is Mrs. Griffin. Mrs. Walter Griffin. She has sailed with us . . . five times, perhaps six. Over two seasons."

"Can you describe her husband?"

"Oh, yes, of course. A large man, brown, very strong looking. A large jaw, small mouth."

"Have they acted unusual in any way?"

"I would say no, not really. Always the best accomodations, an outside room on the lounge deck. Quiet people. Stay to themselves. A table for two they must have. They do not join in the fun, you know? The poor woman, she cannot take the sunshine, so I wonder why she does go on cruises. He would spend much time in the sun. They are generous with tipping. Is there trouble? Perhaps she is the wife of some other person. Believe me, I could not make any statement about such a thing. We cannot get involved in a thing of that kind. It is not our affair."

"I am not going to ask for a statement."

"There is nothing more I could tell you. I hope I have helped you. Oh, one thing. They have always taken our shorter cruises."

"Where is the *Monica D.* now?"

"On her last Caribbean cruise of this season. We have had our last. Tonight we sail for Italy, perform Mediterranean cruises, and return in late November. The *Monica D.* will join us in the Mediterranean."

He took out a thick black wallet, leafed through some cards, handed me one. "This, sir, is the cruise schedule of both vessels this season. Could you now excuse me, please?"

I stood in the shade of the customs shed and found,

on the card, the final cruise of the season of the *Monica D*. It was a seven-day cruise. She had left Port Everglades last Tuesday at ten o'clock in the evening. She had arrived this same Friday at Kingston, Jamaica, at seven in the morning, and would leave at five in the evening today. Tomorrow she would arrive at Port-au-Prince at one in the afternoon and leave at nine in the evening. On Monday she would arrive at Nassau at one in the afternoon and leave at five o'clock—just four hours later. And dock right back here at eight in the morning next Tuesday.

With Ans Terry and Del aboard. Nice quiet people, who'd keep to themselves and occupy an outside room on the lounge deck and tip generously.

I decided it would be very interesting to fly over to Nassau late Sunday or early Monday and ride back on the *Monica D*. At this time of year they would have available space.

Ans and Del might be a little bored. I might liven up the last leg of the journey. But there was one problem to solve, and if the *Veronica D*. was sailing at five, a little close observation might give me a valuable clue. And it was a situation where I might well use Meyer's disciplined brain.

I found The Hairy One just returning from the beach with two sandy moppets in tow, ages about four and five. He explained that it was a small favor for the mother, a chance for her to go to the hospital to visit the father, who had managed to set up an A-frame to hoist a marine deisel engine up where he could work on it, and then had lowered it onto his right foot.

"It is saddening," he said, "to learn how the young are being deprived of their cultural heritage. This pair had never even heard of Little Red Ridinggoose and the Three Bare Facts."

"He's all mixed up," the little girl explained solemnly.

"He found a penny in my ear," the little boy proclaimed.

He sacked them out in the bunks aboard the *John Maynard Keynes* for the obligatory nap, and I heard him explain solemnly that he wouldn't tell on them if they didn't take their naps, but to keep him from being a bad liar, they had to *look* like people taking naps, so they had to close their eyes, breathe deeply, and make no sound at all for a little while. And as long as they were doing nothing but pretending to take naps, they could be thinking him up a better ending for Little Red Ridinggoose. She deserved better than to be sent off to Yale.

We sat on the cockpit deck under the shade of an awning he had rigged. The sea breeze moved by. We kept our voices down.

I was aware of his careful and intense and questioning stare. He said at last, "You have the look of having felt a stale cold breath on the back of the neck, Travis. The jocular detachment, that look of the bemused spectator has been compromised."

"It got very iffy. It got very close in all respects. Somebody who gives you just one small poor chance is very good indeed, and the him or me rationalization is never totally satisfactory. By dawn's early light I buried him on a beach, in soft sand, using a hunk of driftwood, and it keeps bothering me that I buried him face down. It makes no difference to him. But I keep remembering the look of the back of his neck. The one called Griff. And I am not ready to talk about it. Not for a while. Some night, Meyer, in the right mood, I'll tell you."

"Tell me just one thing now. Will anybody come looking for you?"

"No. He thought it was going to be the other way around. So he made certain nobody would be looking for him. He set it up very nicely. Only the names were changed. And nobody else in the group knows of me or has seen me."

"And there is still the interesting lure of the money, eh?"

"I brought that back."

"So that's the end of it?" The smile on that massive and ugly face was all too knowing.

"That's what I tried to talk myself into."

"But then it would keep going on, wouldn't it?"

"And the shape of it is just about what we guessed, Meyer. I keep picking up more details. And, as a reasonable guess, I think they've murdered between thirty and forty men in the past two years. And it could have been going on before that, before Vangie was recruited."

"I knew the figures would be high."

He surprised me. "How could you know that?"

"We estimated the total take. If any single venture netted a really large amount, there would be people tracking down every tiny clue. Heirs in hot pursuit of money in six figures would be tireless, and able to pay well for expert assistance. But ten or fifteen or twenty thousand . . . there would be less furor, and a much longer list of potential victims. Of course you have one curious problem. You're not so naïve as to appoint yourself an angel of vengeance, burying them in the soft sand, face down, one at a time."

"I have to crack one open. So wide open it will stay open, and then I have to hand it over to a cop bright enough to see what he's got, and I have to do it in such a way that I can melt back into the woodwork. I have two candidates. And a little thought or two for each of them. But let me use you on the one problem that baffles me."

"Only one?"

"Only one at a time, Meyer."

At twenty minutes to five we arrived at dockside in all the confusions of sailing. They were obviously going to have a fairly full ship for the transatlantic run. The literature I had picked up at a travel agency on the way over said the capacity was three hundred plus. Passengers were boarding. They had three gangplanks out. Crew only. Passengers only. Visitors only. We went up the visitors' gangplank. The gate onto the deck was narrow. We were each given a rather dogeared blue card. One crew member gave us our cards and as he did so, he chanted the new head count in Italian, and the crew member standing behind him marked it on a clip-

board. We did not go below. We performed little ex-
periments. We tried to leave by the passenger gangplank and were politely turned back. Meyer asked if
he could leave the ship for a few minutes and keep his
blue card and return. Ah, no sir. It is so easy, just geeve
it now, we geeve it back, eh?

The time grew near. The ship's group of six musicians
stood on one of the lower weather decks, playing sentimental Italian songs of sorrow and parting. People threw
paper streamers. People ashore behind the wire waved
and waved and waved. There was a call for visitors to
leave. And another. And a final call. And we watched
the jam as they surrendered their blue cards, putting
them into the outstretched hand of the crew member.
He would count them in batches, sing out the count, drop
them into a slot in a wooden box as his companion kept
score. Meyer went ashore. I leaned on the rail a dozen
feet from the gangplank. The two crewmen conferred.
The dock crew was beginning to cast off the first lines.
One crew member hurried off.

Over the increased tempo of the music the bull horn
blared, "Please. Your *attencion*! One guest is steel aboard
the sheep. Please, that guest weel go ashore imme-
diately."

So I surrendered my blue card and went ashore, and
the crew member was slightly disapproving of me. They
pulled the gangplank away as soon as I stepped off it.
I found Meyer behind the wire, grinning. He pulled
me away from the people and said, "Very simple, once
you figure it out. It makes you wonder what took you so
long."

"If you try to make me guess, old buddy. . . ."

"Two visitors go aboard. One takes both cards. He
waits for the maximum traffic density of the people
leaving, those times when the card collector accumulates
a stack and counts them during the next lull. They count
cards, not heads. So the two cards, aligned to look like
one, get popped into his outstretched hand. All cards
issued are accounted for. If somebody visiting happens to lose his card while aboard, if it blows over or

something, no sweat. He just says he lost it. They let him off, take him off the count. The system leaves everything tidy. But they sail with one extra. If they had to sail without getting the correct count, there'd be a determined search for a stowaway. They sail with an extra passenger they know nothing about, and in transit, the arithmetic is adjusted back to the proper number. The accomplice cannot come aboard as a passenger, of course. It would distress them to run a short count. It would imply somebody fell overboard."

We turned and watched the *Veronica D.* moving away from the dock. "I could have slipped him both cards," Meyer said, "and you would still be aboard."

That night, up on the sun deck aboard the *Flush,* I told him all of it. All except the Griff part. And I told him the things I thought I might try. And he came up with a few impressive refinements.

Saturday morning, after I had rather unwillingly agreed to a more direct participation on his part, I made the ticket arrangements for us. A flight early Monday morning from Miami to Nassau on Bahamas Airways. And two tickets back to Port Everglades from Nassau on the *Monica D.,* Stateroom Number 6 for me, an outside room on the Lounge Deck. And, for Meyer, the most remote thing I could find, according to the chart of the ship, an inside room on B Deck. There were only ten staterooms on B Deck, and those were clustered in the stern section. He got Number 215, a cubicle with a bed and pullman upper, a shower and a toilet.

We then went to see an old friend of mine named Jake Karlo. No one knows his age. He is about the size of a full-grown cricket. His standard gait is a jog trot. He has kept up with the changing times. When I first knew him he had a tiny office in a ratty old building in one of the oldest parts of downtown Miami. He booked third-class talent into fourth-class saloons—beefy strippers, loud young unfunny comedians and loud old unfunny comedians, off-key sopranos for weddings, and off-key baritones for funerals, musicians who would take years to make it, and musicians who had made it too long ago, butterfingered jugglers, trained dogs and shabby chorus lines. But he could make you believe each act was the greatest.

Now he has an office layout of such size, elegance and persuasion it is sometimes called Goodson-Todman South. He owns substantial percentages of several successful clubs, a piece of a theater chain, a big interest in a television production company, and a hundred per cent of both an equipment rental firm and a big commercial color lab. With the steady growth of the Miami area as a moving picture and television center, Jake has maneuvered himself into a position where he can supply all the necessary production equipment, furnish all necessary technicians, build and rent sets, supply people for bit parts and for use as extras, costume them, and process the film for final editing.

Several years ago several con artists moved in on him, set him up beautifully, bled off his working capital, then moved in closer to bail him out in return for control. Somebody recommended me. I had to get Jake to imitate total defeat, and when their guard dropped and they began congratulating each other, we worked our own con game on them. Jake has not forgotten.

He came running across his half acre of carpeting. I introduced him to Meyer. Jake leaned back on his heels and stared up at me, like a man admiring a tall building. "Mr. Meyer," he said, "how this monster saved my life, believe me! Thieves from the Coast in black neckties, they knew everything. They knew how to peel poor old Jake Karlo like a banana. So what problems could they have with a type like this McGee? Such a big rugged honest one, like they would cast him in westerns, and actors those people eat for breakfast. When they left, maybe it was by Greyhound bus. All we let them keep was the cufflinks and the black neckties, heh? This McGee, he never comes to see an old man just for friendship. Always some favor. What is it now? Jake Karlo's right arm? All you do is ask, it's yours."

"Meyer," I said, "you will never believe it, but this active young man has twenty-one grandchildren."

"Twenty-three. Keep track, at least. But not one with the name. Every one we had was a girl yet. Six of them. Who gets the name? My brother's boy. Such a genius! Seven jobs I try him in. Even emptying wastebaskets, he could find some way to cost me a thousand dollars an hour. Come on. Sit, gentlemen. I told them out there, no calls, no interruptions."

I told him what I wanted, and he spread out the four photographs of Vangie, the five by sevens. He sat behind his giant desk and looked at them with pursed lips.

"You look," he said, "you say lovely. Oval face, delicacy, some oriental blood. Absolutely great eyes. Then more and more you keep seeing animal. Like a warning there. Watch out. How about the size, the build?"

"About five seven. Hundred and twenty to twenty-five. But the kind of body that looks riper than the weight. Physical condition of a dancer."

He nodded. "Sure. One kid I've got, she's five foot and doesn't go a hundred pounds. Not really so much upstairs or downstairs, but what gives it that look, the waist is practically nothing. You've got with her a fourteen-inch difference from waist to hips, nineteen to thirty-three. She's doing a fishbowl at the Shoreliner, and the bar business, it's making everybody rich, just when the smart money figured the fishbowl bit was dead forever."

Seeing the puzzlement on Meyer's face, I said, "A nude girl dances very slowly, making sort of swimming motions, in a little brightly lighted room directly under the bar. Mirrors reflect the image of her, only about four inches tall, into fishbowls full of water spaced along the bar. It's an effective illusion. Jake, have you got anybody who might fit the bill?"

"How close does she have to work? What'll the lighting be?"

"Daylight, but a long way off. Say a hundred feet."

"So the face is important, but what has got to be right is posture, the way she moves, the way she walks." He pressed the lever on his intercom and said, "Liz, bring me in the specialty book, the one the cover is green on."

In a few moments the secretary came in and put a thick album bound in green leather in front of her diminutive boss. He flipped the pages rapidly. The photographs were eight-by-ten glossies, in clear acetate sleeves, with the pertinent information about each one on the facing page.

He stopped at one, studied it, held Vangie's picture beside it, looked from one to the other and said, "Just right."

He spun the book around and we stared at it and saw a smiling, clear-faced, brown-eyed, Nordic blonde.

"Is this a rib?" I asked him.

He stood up, leaned across the desk, pointed the features out one by one, with an air of great patience. "Shape of the face. High cheekbones. Same type mouth. Same type eyes once Kretoffski gets through with her. How many wigs we own? Maybe two thousand? So relax. Read the stats."

Miss Merrimay Lane. Twenty-three, Five seven. One twenty-three. Specialty dancer: Interpretive, comedy, acrobatic, tap, chorus, exotic.

"A dancer is best," Jake said. "Body control. This chick was working on the Beach, then they closed out for the season May fifteen. Let's hope she stayed put." He gave his secretary the phone number.

After a few minutes, at the sound of a little musical bong, Jake lifted the phone and in a slower and deeper voice said, "Merrimay, sweetheart! Would you be free for a little daytime one-shot?" He listened, winked at me, and said, "Darling girl, don't you know by now that Uncle Jake will squeeze the client for the final peso? No, dear. Not dancing. No audition required. So wrap something around it, precious girl, and put it in a cab and hustle it on down here to my office. Twenty minutes? You are such a delight, I mean it, dear." He hung up and spoke into the box, telling his secretary to get Kretoffski to report to him in thirty minutes.

He looked at me and said, "Boychick, an arm you can have. A leg you can have. But one of my people getting hurt? That's out."

"Did you have to say that, Jake?"

"For the record only."

"She starts work in Lauderdale at eight o'clock Tuesday morning. But I want to take her up there for a briefing tomorrow. There's an off-chance she might have to go with me up to Broward Beach sometime on Tuesday or Wednesday. But that will be it. How does five hundred sound, plus expenses?"

"In January, February, it isn't such great arithmetic. In June it is a lover's kiss."

Merrimay Lane was announced and made an extravagant entrance. She came sweeping in wearing an orange strapless sunback dress, white gloves, purse and shoes, gigantic false lashes, a cloud of spicy perfume, a funny little hat in orange-colored straw balanced atop blonde tresses. She covered space with the effortless ease of the dancer, made glad cries at Jake, kissed his cheek, whirled and looked with pert expectancy at us.

"The giant there, darling girl, that is Mr. Travis McGee, a very personal dear friend who I would trust with all six of my lovely daughters, if you start thinking anything is strange about what he wants done, you shouldn't worry. And his associate, Mr. Meyer. What I can say is this beautiful young girl is one of the hardest reliable workers you want to meet, strictly pro, and no temper tantrums, and she learns routines like lightning. And what it is he wants you to do, sweetheart, I think afterward you keep your mouth shut. I have people waiting to see me on the next floor down, so the talking you can do here. Feel free. Take your time. When Kretoffski comes, Liz will send him right in."

"Maybe if she could hold him until we cover the part he doesn't have to know?"

"On the way out, I will tell her that."

When the door shut, Merrimay said, "Well, it certainly sounds terribly mysterious."

I handed her one of the pictures of Vangie. "You have

to be mistaken for this girl, at a distance, a good distance, in daylight."

She studied it, turned her head this way and that.

"Hmm. If my mother had married a Chinese, or a half Chinese. My size?"

"Very close."

"I suppose the big question is why."

I had delayed making up my mind until that moment, but I had respect for the intelligence I saw in her eyes. "Some people tried to kill her. It was a very good try. They thought they had. She had a miraculous escape. So when she showed up again, it had to be a very nasty shock. They made absolutely certain the next time. So if one of them should see her again . . . we might make some good use of the reaction."

She stared at me, swallowed visibly, put her fingertips to her throat. "Couldn't it turn out to be a nasty shock to me, too?"

"There'll be no way for him to get near you. That is absolutely guaranteed. You'll understand when we show you the physical layout. And if at that point, you want to say no, you'll still get the five hundred."

She looked at the picture again. "She's very interesting looking. But it is sort of a cheap pose, actually. Do you know how she held herself, how she walked, all that?"

"Mr. Meyer and I spent two days with her."

"She was about twenty-five?"

"Twenty-six."

"What did she do?"

"She'd been a prostitute for twelve years."

Merrimay's brown eyes widened. "My word, that's quite an early start, isn't it?"

"For a time she was a five-hundred-dollar call girl in New York."

She looked incredulous. "They make *that* much?"

"A few of them."

She shrugged. "Okay, then. It's a deal, provided I can back out if there's something I don't want to do. But I don't want to know any more about her until Si Kretoff-ski gets me fixed up."

"The sun poisoned her," Meyer said. "She was quite pale."

"I can see that. It's no problem. What about clothes?"

"I think," Meyer said, "what she was wearing the first time they tried." He looked at me and I nodded. "Miss Lane, it was an oyster white wraparound skirt in that Orlon fleece material, and a sleeveless blouse, raw silk, natural, with sort of a Chinese collar effect in front, and cut halfway down the back, a circular cut."

She frowned. "Wardrobe might have it. How much time is there?"

"It will happen early Tuesday morning."

"Oh, then if they don't have it, I can find something close enough. You'll pay expenses?"

"Of course."

By quarter of five that Saturday afternoon, we were ready to demonstrate the final result to Jake Karlo.

Merrimay wanted time to freshen her make-up, so we went to Jake's office. Meyer said, "Mr. Karlo, you have some fantastic talents available to you. And that girl may be better than you know. I am exhausted. She bled us of every shred of information. Every habitual gesture we could remember. She even worked on the voice, saying that she knew she wouldn't need it, but it would make her *feel* more like the other girl. Travis, she deserves a bonus."

"Approved."

She tapped on the door and came in. The clothing was almost exact, and the shoes she had picked to go with it were what I could imagine Vangie picking. Kretoff-ski had worked a miracle on her eyes. Only the color was wrong, too deep and soft a brown.

It was Vangie's walk, that tautly controlled sway, swing and tilt of hip, toeing in slightly. It was Vangie's pallor, and her way of looking at you, head lowered, a look of brooding challenge. She tilted her head to thumb back a wing of the dark hair, and, pitching her voice deeper, she came very close to achieving that same richness.

She stood, hipshot, in front of the desk. "They said you boys wanted me in here. I'm Vangie, it's short for Evangeline. Bellemer. Honest to God, it's getting to be a real drag hanging around here the whole damn day long, I mean I'm like used to more action." She turned away, did a vague slow dance step, turned and dropped into a chair and scowled at us. "Trav, honey, the very least you could do is break out some good bourbon for Vangie, I mean it's coming up that time of day, isn't it?" She ran her tonguetip along her underlip. I'd seen Vangie do that, just as slowly, forty times.

It wasn't quite right, of course. She wasn't Vangie, but she was so close, so heartbreakingly close it chilled the nape of my neck. I hadn't realized how much all that hard work had accomplished.

Jake tore a sheet of paper off his desk pad, folded it once and held it up. "Sweetheart, I have written a word on this piece of paper. It is a word of great meaning. It is a word I have respected all my life. I am a fool This word was in front of me and I couldn't read it. Monday it will be added to your file, lovely girl. Later in the week we will take new pictures of you " He trotted over to her. "I give you this piece of paper. Jake Karlo never writes anything foolish about something so great and wonderful and beautiful."

She opened the piece of paper. She stared up at him with Vangie's mocking smile. "Actress! Where have you been, honey? Don't they let you out? Listen, you want to turn a five-hundred-dollar trick and have the john ask for you the next time he hits town, you *got* to be an actress. Right?"

Jake, beaming, turned and held his arms wide. "See? See?"

"Jake, darling," she said. "Please don't. You'll make me cry, and it will spoil the eyes. And . . . all day I've been getting closer and closer to tears. For Vangie, I guess. There but for the grace of God, or something. The poor, sad, simple bitch. Jake, you make me very happy. Damn, damn, damn. I'm going to cry." She got up and ran out of the room.

"We can use her a lot closer than I'd have thought possible," I said.

"Not too close," Jake said. "Not close to trouble." He thumped the desk top with his little fist. "A man gets so busy he doesn't look good at his own people. A sweet child like that, all of a sudden a hundred and ten per cent floozy. And she photographs like a dream. If she doesn't freeze up, if she doesn't choke when the lights go on, I can merchandise that dear little package. Discipline she's got. What I got to do is set up a test, something where say she's dancing, she comes running off stage, big applause. She's happy. The guy is waiting there. He tells her something that breaks her heart. She gives it a very slow take. She can't believe it. Then say she thinks it's a joke and tries to laugh. Extreme closeup. Say she's just made it. Real big. And the tests have come back. Leukemia." He hit the desk again. "A take like that, in ten minutes I can sell her to Max on a seven-year deal, script approval, good options. I make her twenty-one years old. Merrimay Lane. It sounds *good*. Already you can hear it's got star quality."

Though he said goodby to us, and walked us to the elevators, I had the feeling we were getting not more than ten per cent of his attention.

On the fast ride down I said to Meyer, "Was she that good?"

"Believe me, boychick, the broad was colossal."

ELEVEN

AT TEN-THIRTY on that hot bright breezy Monday morning, the black taxi brought us in from the airport, down Nassau Street and east on Bay Street, to let us off at Rawson Square. I knew from the look of Bay Street that no cruise ships were in. In the hot months when there are no cruise ships tied up at Prince George Wharf or anchored out in the harbor beyond the lighthouse, Bay Street slows to a walk. The pretty little shopgirls stroll and chatter. Drivers in their cabs. Traffic is sparse and stately. The fat dark women yawn and gossip in the straw markets as they weave the tourist goods.

It is the rest period for that big machine which is Bay Street. The components of the machine are the heavily stocked shops with luxury items from all over the world. Solomon's Mines, Trade Winds, John Bull, Cellars Wineshop, the Island Shop, the English China House, Kelly's, Lightbourns, M'Lords, Mademoiselle, The Nassau Shop, the Perfume Box, Robertson and Symonette, Sue Nan's, Vanity Fair.

A quiet time, when the locals can shop in thoughtful and leisurely relaxation, and when the long bars in Dirty Dick's, the Junkanoo and Blackbeard's Tavern are empty.

We walked past the straw market and the rental boats out to the wharf area, carrying our minimal luggage.

"I never really believed you'd ever take me on a cruise, dear," Meyer said.

"How did you get so lucky?"

I found an official-looking mustachioed fellow who

told me that the *Monica D.* would tie up at the wharf about one o'clock, and a Dutch boat was due in the evening. We checked the bags at the Prince George Hotel, and then we went shopping for some little remembrance for Ans Terry and his lady. Meyer was dubious about our being able to find anything of sufficient symbolic impact. I said we'd look around, buy what we found and then, after meeting the gentleman, decide whether or not it was reasonable to expect a useful reaction. The more off balance he was by tomorrow morning, the more deadly would be the effect of seeing Vangie.

It was Meyer who spotted the display of dolls in a case in Solomon's Mines, beckoned me over and pointed one out. Dolls of all nations. And the Japanese one bore a faint resemblance to Vangie. She was about five inches tall, beautifully made. The clerk took it out of the case for us. Black hair was glued in place, and the kimono was sewn on. We bought it. At Kelly's Hardware we bought a spool of fine wire, a piece of soft sculptor's stone, a file and a carving knife.

We repaired to the pleasantly dark bar at the Carlton House on East Street. When the bartender had fixed us each one of their superb planter's punches and moved away, Meyer said, "I am extremely nervous, Trav. This is a long way from economic theory. I'm certain I'm going to make some terrible blunder."

I realized he could not function in a vacuum and play it by ear as we went along. People need an identity, a place to stand. I said, "McGee and Meyer are both from Fort Lauderdale. They came over separately. Meyer had some talks with people on the Nassau Development Board about the economic consequences of a change in the corporate tax structure or some damn thing, at your usual per diem and expenses. McGee came over with a batch of people joining a big party going on at Paradise Beach and now that the party is running out of charge, he's heading home. We ran into each other on Bay Street. We're casual acquaintances. We're going back on the same ship, but you bore me. I'm more interested in lining up some dainty lollipop. Maybe I can get some mileage out of you by sticking your thumb in Ans Terry's buttonhole while I cut his lollipop out of the pack. Or maybe it might work the other way. The legendary Meyer charm might work well on the lollipop, while I trick Ans into going down to your squalid accommodations where I can thump his head and lace him to your bunk. Anyway, we establish a message center and get to work giving them the eerie feeling there is something gone wrong in the world, a warp in reality, some cogs slipping in their skulls. They're ice cold, Meyer. Heartless and murderous. But any savage animal gets bad nerves when confronted with the inexplicable. We just give them a Halloween party, with a few goblins to think about."

"That particular smile, McGee. I am very glad you have no good reason to come looking for one Meyer. Okay, I feel better. Skoal!"

We stood in the dusty shade and watched them, with casual skill, latch the *Monica D.* to the wharf. She was dressed up to come in, flapping with as many pennants and flags and banners as three new gas stations on opening day. Deck crew in whites, and the packed, expectant, gaudy, gabbling pack of passengers crowding the starboard side of B Deck where the gangplank would be affixed. This was the last romantic port of call, and I could well imagine that their cruise director had made some dampening comments about shopping on Bay Street. This is standard procedure. The cruise directors hawk the marvels of the wares at those ports where they have set up a kickback from the shops. At St. Thomas and Curaçao and Kingston the cruise directors give glowing recommendations about specific shops. But they can't pry any kickbacks out of Bay Street because it is too well, too solidly established, too world renowned to give a hoot. The big machine chews up the people, but it gives fair value.

Four hours ashore at the mercy of the machine. Five big taxis were waiting, an indication that there were a few who had signed up for a tour of the island.

The chain was dropped, and as the harried staff

checked them off, the folk came hurrying down the gang-plank. In the lead was an overstrength platoon of the same beefy and resolute women you see bursting into department stores on sale days the instant the doors are unlocked. Great hams bulged the lurid shorts.

"Attention please, attention please. Passengers taking the tour will please board the limousines off to your left as you debark. Thank you."

The ship's last cruise of the season, a short one, at the lowest rates. Yet it was at only a little more than half capacity, they had told me. During the height of the season, in the first three months of any year, when these small cruise ships that ply the Caribbean are at capacity, a good two-thirds of the passenger list is made up of what a friend of mine who worked aboard one for a season called the "mother" trade. To explain what he meant, he would give you a big expansive smile and say, "I always promised mother that some day I'd take her on a cruise. Well, sir, with the kids married off and the store sold, I said to her, I said, 'Mother, you better start packing, because we're a-going on that cruise.' "

So they fill up the little ships, eat the spiced and stylized cruise food, get seasick, sunburned. They take afternoon dance lessons in the Neapolitan Ballroom, play organized deck games, splosh about in the small pool on the sundeck, play bridge, get a little tiddly and giggly, dress up for dinner and appraise the dresses of the other women, get totally confused about which port is which, take fragmentary language lessons, vigorously applaud the meager talents of the ship's floor show, take all the tours, write and mail scores of postcards, compete for prizes in the costume ball, spend a dutiful amount of time each day at sea in the rental deck chair.

In the brochures, of course, there were the beautiful people dancing gracefully and romantically by moonlight and the light of Japanese lanterns on the tropic deck of a brand new ship, and the same lovely people smiling in the warm sunlight, their golden limbs in relaxed and effective composition around the blue dance of the huge shipboard swimming pool.

It isn't like that. These little ships are lumpy with end-less coats of topside paint, and the ship's staff is over-worked, and the schedules are rigidly set, with brassy announcements coming over the speaker systems, send-ing the whole herd moving in one direction or another.

It isn't like they thought. But it isn't like anything else they ever knew either. Perhaps, in some wistful and tender sense, these *are* the beautiful people, and because this is the dream fulfilled, they hold onto it tightly, mak-ing small translations from reality. And down there, in the cramped inconveniences of the little cabins, in the slightly oily wind of the ship's airconditioning, in the muted grumble of the ship's engines, the little vibra-tional shudders as she crosses the tropic ocean, sun-burned flesh is coupled in a passion more like that of years ago, and in the breakfast morning they smile into each other's eyes, a secret recognition.

But this was the tag end of the season, and a mixed bag. Scampering flocks of small children. A sprinkling of heavy men in their middle years, accompanying, with a certain air of apprehension, their young doughy blondes toward the Bay Street shops. A contingent of scrubbed-looking highschool kids chaperoned by a nervous-acting couple who looked like a male and female Woodrow Wilson, and an unchaperoned pack of kids of college age, the girls like a bright fluttering flock of tropic birds, the boys languid under the terrible burden of improvised sophistication, and thirty or forty couples of the "mother" classification.

The tour caravan left. The others dispersed into Bay Street. The machine came to life. It could readily chew up the entire passenger lists of four deluxe cruise ships simultaneously, each one better than twice the size of the little *Monica D*. The saloons turned the music on. The straw market women began their sales patter, wav-ing the merchandise, and making crude comment on the Jamaican hats a lot of cruise people were wearing. These people were a tiny morsel for the machine, a hundred and fifty or so, but with proper pressure, calibration, alignment of the rollers and levers and sluice gates, it might churn eight thousand dollars out of this motley group, and there was little else to do on a Monday afternoon in June anyway.

The mystique of the operation is that a true blue consumer will buy something she does not need and cannot afford when she discovers that the same item at home would cost her thirty dollars more.

Our targets were not in the pack, and just as I was about to say we'd better go aboard, she started slowly down the gangplank. Unmistakably she. Theatrically she, making her exit after the rabble had been cleared from her path.

White cotton twill pants, fitting her slenderness with an almost improbable snugness. They came to just above her bare ankles, with a slight flare, an instep notch. The wide waistband was snugged around her slender waist, and above it was six supple bare inches of midriff, and above that a little half-sleeve truncated blouse, fine red and white stripes, so dense with stiff ruffles she looked like a Christmas display of ribbon candy. Atop the interwoven and intricate coiffure of cream-blonde hair was perched at a perfect straightness a wide-brimmed, white bullfighter hat of straw in a fine weave, with white ball fringe dangling all the way around the rim. She carried a red purse shaped like a lunch bucket. Her sandals had half-heels, white straps, thick cork soles. The very wide flat rims of her sunglasses had a red and white checkerboard pattern.

She came slowly down the incline of the gangplank, the slope creating, with the thick soles of the sandals, considerably more hip motion than she could have achieved on a level surface. Every crew member who could get to a rail on the starboard side stopped all work and watched the descent. The only discernible flaw in her figure was that her thighs, as revealed by the tightness of the pants, were too long and too heavy to be in proportion to the rest of her. She was slightly tanned, just enough to set off the smoothness between waistband and blouse. I could sense the concerted inaudible sigh as she reached the level of the cement dock. She walked with a sense of complete awareness of being watched, looking straight ahead, undeviatingly. It was a triumph of merchandising, a perfect gem of functional display techniques, as specific as the cutaway working models of engines at auto shows. She turned and looked back up at the deck. A big man appeared and came down toward her. He had a long, limber stride, a small waist and hips under white stretch Levis, and great wads of muscle bulging the navy blue knit sports shirt. His pale forearms had almost the exaggerated meatiness of Popeye the Sailor, and he held himself and moved in a way that betrayed those curious anxieties of the Mr. America syndrome. He had a face far older than the body, long, eroded and sallow, with brows and lashes of such pallor it had an expressionless look. There was something just wrong enough about his pale curly locks to make me quite certain it was a hairpiece. A long slim cigar was clamped at an uptilted angle in the corner of his mouth. The girl had continued walking, and when he caught up with her, they stopped and talked. She tilted her head back so she could look up at him from under the hat brim. Seeing them together I realized he was big enough to look me in the eye.

She took a list from her purse. He looked at it with her. He shrugged, tapped ash from the cigar, walked with her toward Bay Street.

I got my bag from the hotel and went aboard first, presented my ticket, was properly greeted.

"I saw that couple come off several minutes ago, and they looked familiar. Both of them in white pants."

"Ah, Mr. and Mrs. Terry. Yes, of course. They have traveled with us before. You know them?"

"The name doesn't sound right. I guess I'm mistaken."

"You will have a chance to see them more closely, perhaps. You are almost neighbors. They are also on the port side, also in an outside cabin on the lounge deck. Number fourteen, several rooms forward of yours, sir."

There was no one at the steward's station and no sign of a maid. I located the key rack, opened the glass door and took the key to six from its hook. The cabin was bright and pleasant. I checked the location of fourteen and went, as planned, to the ship's lounge. The ceiling, of white pegboard, wasn't high enough for me. It would be all too easy to tear my scalp on one of the little round sprinkler heads which protruded from it. There were groupings of overstuffed chairs and sofas, upholstered in blue, yellow, rose and purple, surrounding round black tables with raised chrome edges. The floor was of black composition. I picked a group with yellow upholstery, and had a waiter bring me a Pauli Girl beer. From time to time a passenger would hurry through, all haste, frowns and concentration, camera clanking.

Meyer appeared, sat down with a heavy sigh. "I am entombed down there, in a ghastly flickering glow of tiny light bulbs." He pointed aft. "I have our mail drop. The first stairway through that door, halfway down, at the curve, a fire hose in a case. The top is recessed a little. So, the top right corner of it, the right as you face it."

"Very good."

"And it has struck me that we might make use of the PA system. I have heard them paging people."

"Also very good, depending. I'm off. She had a list. So it's an odds-on chance they split up. Go play with your doll."

At almost two-thirty I spotted her, alone, just going into the Nassau Shop, carrying one dressbox-size package. I followed her in. She put the sunglasses in her purse. She strolled slowly back through the store and stopped at a circular rack containing Daks skirts. I was loafing about eight feet away when the clerk approached her.

When she spoke I learned she had a child voice, a little thin dear girlie voice. "This one, in the green, this is just linen, isn't it? No other fabric to keep it from wrinkling?"

"Pure linen, miss."

"So you put it on and an hour later it looks like you'd slept in it. No thanks."

"A beautiful wool, perhaps, miss? In this soft gray?"

"I guess not. Thanks anyhow."

I circled and came upon her at the end of a counter, face to face, glance to glance in the instant of passing, sensed behind her eyes the little click of appraisal and dismissal, as if back in there was mounted one of the tired old cameras used by defeated photographers on the littered boardwalks of unfashionable resorts.

Hers was a pointy little face under the bulk of hat and weight of hair. The fur of her eyebrows angled up in a habitual query that no longer asked any questions. It was a small mouth, with the pulp of the unpainted lips so bulgingly, ripely plump she had the look of getting ready to whistle. Sharp little nose and sharp little chin, and an angled flatness in her cheeks. The feature that unified all the rest of it was the eyes, very very large, widely set, brilliantly and startlingly green. She was all erotic innocence and innocent eroticism, moving by me, knowing I would turn to stare, that I would see the arrogance, the slow laziness, the luxurious challenge of the lazy scissors of the long weight of white thighs and the soft flexing perkiness of the little rump. She made me think of a Barbie Doll.

I did not know what to try or how to try it. I could not appraise how much nerve she had or how much intelligence. Nor how completely Terry owned her. If, by luck, I rested the edge of the wedge at exactly the right point, tapped with proper impact, the crystalline structure might cleave. More probably any attempt would glance off, arouse suspicion, send her trotting to wherever Ans Terry awaited her, with a description of me. But if she could be convinced, very quickly, that she was marked for execution also. . . . I had to stake the whole thing on how much she knew about what had happened to Tami. Then I found one possible way I could do it, with a fair chance of its working.

She had gone to a counter where, under glass, elegant little Swiss watches were displayed. The clerk helping her went off to get something out of stock. I moved quickly to stand beside her and said in a low voice, "If you're Del Whitney, I have to talk to you. I've got a message from Tami."

"You've got me confused with somebody. Sorry."

"Tami gave me the message before they killed her, and she told me how I could find you."

Out of the corner of my eye I saw her turn to stare up at me from under the flat brim of the hat. I turned my head slightly, looked at her, saw her absolute rigidity, eyes made even larger by shock. The clerk was returning. "K-k-killed!" she whispered. I had that same feeling you get in a hand of stud poker when you've hung in there with sevens back to back, seen the third one go elsewhere, debate hanging in there with those two kings staring at you across the table, then meet the raise and see the case seven hit you, and know then just how you are going to play it.

"Is this what you had in mind, miss?" the clerk asked.

"What? No. No, thank you." She moved away from the counter and, ten feet away, stopped and stared at me again. I could sense that she was beginning to suspect she had been tricked and had responded clumsily.

"I don't think it would be smart for Terry to see us together." I took out my wallet, felt in the compartment behind the cards, pulled out the folded clipping of the report of the fingerprint identification. "If you didn't happen to know her by this name, Del, it won't mean much."

She unfolded it. Suddenly her hands began an uncontrollable trembling. The dressbox slipped from under her arm and fell to the carpeting. "Oh God! Oh dear Jesus God!" Her voice had a whistly sound.

I picked up her package. "Pull yourself together! You'll bitch us both up. If you want to stay alive, settle down, damn it. Where's Terry?"

"Wuh-wuh-waiting for me at that Blackbeard thing."

"We better get you a drink."

I took her to the Carlton. Her walk was strange, rigid, made stilt-like by shock. I took her to a dim back corner of the paneled bar lounge, empty at that hour. I got her a double Scotch over ice. She gulped it down and then began to cry, fumbling tissue out of her red purse. She cried almost silently, hunched, shuddering and miserable. At last she mopped her eyes, blew her nose, straightened with a slight shudder.

"I just don't understand. Who are you? What's happening?"

"They tried to kill her. They missed. She came to me. I'm just an old friend she could trust, that's all. I live in Lauderdale. She couldn't take the risk of trying to contact you and DeeDee, so she made me promise to try. DeeDee has disappeared. If you want a good guess, they've knocked her in the head and planted her out in the boondocks someplace."

"My God! What are you trying to *do* to me!"

"Lower your voice! I'm trying to give you Tami's message. She was going to make a run for it. You can see she didn't get into the clear. She tried to sneak back to pick up the money she had stashed away, and probably ran into Griff, whoever he is. She was afraid of running into him. She said to tell you to run. She said that all of a sudden they found out the law was getting too close, and they decided to close out the operation. And because you three hustlers are the way they'd tie the others into it, and because it is a murder ring situation, they made a policy decision to kill the three of you. And it looks as if you're the only one left, Del."

"But they . . . wouldn't!"

"Read the clipping. Kiddy, they hit her so hard with that murder car it splashed her up against the second story of a stone building." When I saw the sickness, I followed it up by taking her wrist and saying, "It smashed one whole side of her head flat, all the way to her nose. And from the waist down she was just a sack of busted meat."

She gagged, swallowed and said, "But I'd find out about it when . . ."

"When you get back? Who'll give you a chance to read last week's newspapers? They'll turn you off before you can unpack, lay low a few months, then recruit new girls."

"I've got to tell Ans! We've got to get away from here!"

I bore down on her slender wrist until pain changed the shape of her mouth. "Smarten up fast, or I can't help you, kiddy. That Monday night before you sailed, dear old Ans wired a cement block to Tami's ankles and heaved her off a highway bridge below Marathon. It was after midnight. Mack drove the car. She was conscious. What they didn't know, there were fishermen under the bridge. They got her up in time. She came to me in Lauderdale. Here I am taking this lousy risk of getting mixed up in this stinking thing, and you come on stupid. They thought she'd be dead. They talked in front of her. Griff and Ans made a sentimental deal. Ans was to drown Tami, and in return Ans turns you over to Griff. Tami said please warn you without Ans knowing. I owed her the favor. She was shook. She'd been sunk into twenty feet of black water with her ankles wired. So I flew over here and I'm booked back on the *Monica D.* I didn't know I'd locate you ashore, from Tami's description. Maybe even with a warning you don't stand a chance. But I made the try. Stay stupid and you're soon dead, because you've been in a business where that's the only way they retire you, sweetie."

It glazed her. She stared wide-eyed into the middle distance, the fat little mouth agape, exposing the gleamings of even little white teeth.

"He's been acting so funny," she whispered. "Jumpy. Cross all the time. And there wasn't any other cruise he drank so much. And mean to me this trip. Nasty mean. He gave me such a thumping! The thing that started it, I asked him when we could quit. First it was going to be just three or four. Then it got up to ten. And this was number fourteen and I said to him that no matter how smooth it went, if you kept it up and kept it up, you were pushing your luck. I said I was getting sick of having such a strain all the time, and how much better everything was when there was just the two of us in the little apartment in Coral Gables, and I worked the conventions over on the Beach. That was no real reason for the thumping he gave me. He's had lots better reasons. I've been with him seven years. This is big money, but . . . when I can't sleep, sometimes I keep thinking about those poor guys. I just can't believe Ans would . . . let them do that to me."

"No, of course not. He is a very sentimental guy. He wants to keep you alive and well, so the cops can pick you up and let a whole swarm of people make identifications, so they can bring you to trial for murder first and let you make a deal with the law and help them nail everybody else. Use your head, kiddy. They know Dee-Dee would make a deal. Vangie would make a deal. Why should they trust the third hooker to keep her mouth shut?"

She bit down on her thumb knuckle. "Tuesday morning it was, he didn't get back to the place until way after three. Then he sat out there drinking, and he wouldn't come to bed. You know . . . I guess it would really bother him to have to do that to Tami. I guess it was hard on him."

"And Griff is going to cry real tears when he tucks you into some swamp."

She shuddered. "Please stop doing that, huh? I have to think. God, I don't know what to do. You can guess how much bread Ans lets me have. I don't have a hundred dollars in the world. I've never been on my own at all. I've been with Ans since I was sixteen. I was third runner-up for Miss Oceanside Beach and he was third runner-up for Mr. Body. He was twennyseven. We teamed up like to help each other, and we went a billion miles in that old car I bet, just barely making out on the contests, a whole year of it, and then he got so sick there in Chicago, and I was working waitress and telling my troubles to a girlfriend, how he was in a charity ward, and the medicines so expensive, and my feet hurting all the time from those damn tile floors, and then my waitress girlfriend took me on that double date, and the guy put fifty bucks into my purse, under the table."

She shook her head slowly, frowning. "When he found out for sure about the hustling, it racked him up. He cried and cried. When he got better we tried to make it the square way, him pumping gas but he got an allergy and his hands swelled so bad he couldn't work, and I went back to hustling, and it didn't bother him so much, and finally it didn't bother him at all."

She frowned at me and said, "He's weak, kind of. He's scared. He could do that to Tami from being scared. It must be killing him inside to think I've got to be killed too. That's why he's so mean and jumpy and drinking and all. . . ." The tiny childish voice trailed off. In the quiet of the empty lounge she sat with head lowered, hat brim concealing her face. Her hand, resting inert next to the ashtray, was small, plump, with short fingers and a thick palm, the nails nibbled so close to the quick her fingertips looked deformed. She wore a narrow gold wedding ring set with small diamond chips, and a little gold wristwatch shaped like a heart, the strap fashioned of thin black fabric cords. It had shifted from its customary position and I could see where the light tan of the wrist surrounded the pattern of a heart in the white untanned skin.

The wrist of a woman and the small tidy forearm always seem to me to have some tender and touching quality, a vulnerable articulation unchanged from the time she was ten or twelve, perhaps the only part of her that her flowering leaves unchanged.

The shaded light was on the paneled wall above us, the glow of it yellow-orange. She turned her head toward me, looked up from under the white straw brim, green eyes in shadow.

"He knows I didn't want to get into this. But what he had done, you see, he had listened to too much about it, and they told him that we knew so much it wouldn't be healthy not to get into it. I guess it isn't so healthy now. Not for anybody. I bet he knows what he can expect too. It could be making him drink so much. He's always been too proud of his body to drink so much. If they're closing the store, how long will Ans and Frankie Loyal last?"

"She didn't mention Frankie."

"He works with DeeDee. Worked with DeeDee. He's more like Ans, sort of. Jittery, kind of nervous about the whole deal. Griff is different. He's closer to Mack and Nogs. Griff is more like helping run the thing, and he worked with Mack and Nogs before, and I think he gets cut in on all three teams too. There's one thing about Griff, he isn't nervous about a thing. A person to him is a bug, and if it is where your foot comes down, that's the way it crumbles. At least, if he gets me, he will make it just as easy for me as he can. I know that. He's always liked me. He's hinted a couple of times we could change the teams around."

"What kind of a name is Nogs?"

"I don't know his real first name. It's some kind of a joke about eggnogs and a Christmas party years and years ago. Nogs Berga is his whole name. I heard Mack say Nogs has a lot of things going for him, a lot of them straight things, like monkey jungles and 'gator farms and frontier towns, and Mack runs our operation for him, getting the credit reports on the guys we line up, and saying what boat to get the tickets on, and fixing it so the postcards get mailed from faraway places from those guys so it won't be a lot of guys disappearing from around this area, which could make a lot of heat after a while. What am I going to do? What do you think I should do?"

"Can you handle yourself so Ans won't suspect you know?"

She gave me a quick glance, with an ugly twist to her fatty little mouth. "There's been plenty I haven't wanted him to suspect, friend."

"But if he does and thumps it out of you, it could put me in the bag, Del."

She shrugged. "I'd tell him I was in a place where a radio was on Miami news, and I heard about Tami and DeeDee and figured it out from the funny way he's acting. Anyway, if you don't want to, why take the boat?

You found me. You did the favor. I don't even know your name. Fly back."

"The name is Travis McGee, and I am in Stateroom Six on the Lounge Deck, and I can give you one idea of what you could do. Will he drink enough to pass out?"

"That's the way it's been going this trip, and he's getting a good start while we're talking."

"Leave him a note. Say you heard the Miami news and figured it out. So you've decided to go over the rail. That would cover you in case Griff has orders to meet the ship and take over right away."

"So then what?"

"So then I give a good piece of money to the room steward, and he'll know a way to fix it so you don't have to disembark with the others. We'll give him a reason he can appreciate. Like a husband waiting outside the customs shed with a gun. Ans Terry isn't going to show anybody that note, not with what you say in it. There'll be a short count on the passengers getting off. Short by two, you and me. But the steward can use a piece of his piece of money to keep anybody from getting agitated. Ans will take your stuff off through customs, and I have an acquaintance on board who'll take my gear off. Then when the whole turmoil is over and everybody gone, we walk off."

She took her hat off and laid it aside, patted her hair, stared into her new drink with narrowed eyes, and rattled her fingernails on the black tabletop.

"Sure. He'll show them the note. I didn't get off. So they'll believe it. They'll believe I took a jump. It gives me a chance to run."

"I can give you a start. A couple of hundred bucks."

With eyes still narrow she said, "Why?"

"Favor to Vangie. I promise a favor, I like to go all the way with it."

"She never said anything about knowing anybody named McGee in Lauderdale."

I got the inscribed photograph from the wallet. She studied it. "Like that, huh? Where'd she know you from?"

"Way back."

She handed the photograph back. "What do you do for bread?"

"I call it salesmanship. But sometimes the mark doesn't mind letting his friends and family know how stupid he was, and then they call it extortion or conspiracy to defraud."

"You got a nice tricky way of figuring things out. I guess you'd make out pretty good in con work, looking more like you race boats or build roads or used to play ball or something. Is there any reason you have to stay in Lauderdale?"

"Why?"

"Maybe you could think up something that would use me for bait. God knows I've had enough practice putting on an act for those guys."

"Fourteen acts."

She lifted her shoulders slightly. "I wouldn't want that kind of an ending, not ever again."

"Let me put it this way, Del. I keep things clean. If you try a rough line of work, you take too big a fall if it goes sour. Almost every con operation is a partnership thing. Sure, I could use you. It might be a good time to move along. It would be a good time of year to go up and work the Jersey shore. But what if these people down here found out somehow you got away? Somebody would come after you. I might be crossing a street with you when they run you down. Why should I take a chance like that? And the law isn't going to believe you took the jump. If they are unraveling it, you could be near the top of their list, and there is a large fall for helping a murderer escape."

"I never killed anybody! I couldn't!"

"You just lured them into the situation, so Ans could do it. Fourteen times. They wouldn't electrocute you. Not a pretty young woman. They almost never do. But they'd hang consecutive sentences on you so that the way you'd finally leave would be out the back gate in a box. And I could get five or ten for harboring a fugitive. Kiddy, I'm walking around free as a bird because I don't take bad risks."

She turned completely to face me, fastened her short fingers around my wrist and went to work on me with those green eyes. It was not an unwavering stare. She moved it around, up and down and across, pausing at my eyes each time. She put an old fuzzy edge on the clear silver of her voice.

"Since I was sixteen I've been sizing guys up. The way I am, dear, I got to *belong* to somebody. Ans was weak, and that was why it wasn't ever the greatest. McGee, you threw all this at me fast. I know you're strong. And I know we react good to each other. There's that feeling you can't miss. So the only choice I've got, dear, is you. I've got to trust you. I've got to let you take charge and get me out of this mess. That's the way things are between us, and maybe it comes out better luck than we could guess. What I can be, when I *have* somebody, is absolutely level all the way. I'll help you any way you want help, and food, clothes and a roof is all I'll need. And I swear to God that if anybody finds me, I'll convince them you didn't know a thing about anything. I can be a help. I can do the college girl bit or the housewife bit or the model bit, or be a young widow or whatever. And the day you say go, I'll go. No strings, no tears. So take a chance, huh?"

But I couldn't get fourteen men out of my mind, men who'd been snookered by the business with the eyes, the dear little voice, men who'd sucked at that plump little mouth, been enclosed between the long warm clasp of thighs, men who'd marveled at the luck that had brought them in their middle years the heats and devotions of such a spectacular young girl, and had gone cruising with her and hadn't lived past the first night aboard, to have their reservation taken over by an aging Mr. Body.

"Maybe," I said. "I'll think about it. Maybe I can come up with an idea which will give me some insurance. It's after four now. When can you shake loose from him?"

She forgot the question for a moment. She shook her head. "It's so spooky, thinking about it. My God, him handing me over to Griff just like I've been handing those marks over to him. Everything you say fits, dear.

We gals should have been able to figure it out. If it ever started to go sour, we three would be the first to go. You know, I'm going to miss those kids. We had a lot of laughs."

"What time?"

"Oh, figuring his track record this trip I'd say he'll fold before eleven o'clock. Maybe even before ten."

"Stateroom Six," I said. I rapped my knuckles on the table. Two quick knocks, a pause, two quick ones again. "Knock like that."

It was interesting to me in a clinical way that in the distance from our table to the street door she managed to sway a tautly fabricked hip against me three separate and insistent times, though she'd had no trouble with sway or balance on the way in. With an instant practicality, she'd changed masters. Now it was merely a case of firmly cementing the new relationship in the only way she knew how.

TWELVE

BACK ABOARD at four-thirty, I checked our mail drop and the slip said, "At home."

I went aft and found my way down to his cabin. He opened the door to my knock. "Welcome to steerage," he said. He pointed to the dressing table. I saw the doll. I went over and picked it up. He had carved a rather good cement block. It dangled on the silvery wire an inch below the ankles.

The doll was naked. Any other doll would have been bare, or unclad. But the Japanese artisan who had made this one, even knowing it would be sewed and glued into a kimono, had given a total and humorless attention to detail, making of it a statue rather than a doll. Even the navel was a typically Asiatic little stub, with incised curlicue.

"Couldn't do a damn thing with the hair," he explained. "I had to cut it all off, soak it in hot water, get it straight, glue it back on—I went ashore for the glue—and shape it with my nail scissors."

"It's a beautiful job, Meyer. Absolutely beautiful."

"After I gave her more eyebrows with a little black ink, it turned into a better resemblance."

"It's going to give our boy one hell of a turn."

"How did you make out?"

He sat on the bunk. I straddled the straight metal chair that faced the dressing table. He was a splendid listener —with expressions of great wonderment, surprise, awe,

146

concern, appreciation—and little gasps and grunts and murmurs in all the right places.

"So I stood under the portico and watched her stilt along to Bay Street, knowing she was giving it a little extra something, adding one extra little circular fillip that made everything else work that much harder to keep up. The resplendent officer atop his little box under his umbrella blew the birds out of the trees with his whistle, and stopped every vehicle in the downtown area to let her cross East Street, and a chap in a sun helmet ran full into an old lady with her arms full of packages. He was looking back over his shoulder at the time."

"My God, Travis, what a fantastic gamble!"

"Just the first contact. That was the gamble. From then on I played it the way she was calling it. I had to sense how much she'd swallow and just what things would give it a ring of truth. When it wasn't working just right, I'd move the walnut shells around again. She's what the Limey locals would call a nasty little bit of work. Nastier than our Vangie. She kids herself more than Vangie did. She's perfectly willing to believe Terry'll dump her because she could be talked into dumping him. With a little persuasion, she would have set up a double on this trip. Let Terry drop their pigeon over the side, then hand Terry to Griff on a platter for the same treatment."

"This business of keeping her aboard, and finding a way to take her away with you. I fell off at one of those curves."

"The instructions I'm going to give you right now will give you enough clue so you can climb back on."

He listened with a total attention, and when I was through, he repeated the whole sequence flawlessly. He was a joy to work with.

"But can you make her do it?" he asked.

"The choice is going to look just fine to her."

We saw her at dinner. A gala night. She came in late, sat alone at a table for two. She wore a dark blue sleeve-less bodice in some glittering metallic thread, a lighter blue cummerbund, a white ankle-length skirt that draped handsomely to her walk. I saw her searching for me after she had ordered. We were fifty feet away. Her gaze swept across me, stopped, came back. She held the glance for a moment, and without expression, gave a single almost imperceptible nod.

A little later I looked over and saw a thick-bodied tourist leaning on her table, bending over, talking to her. The dining room lights made a gleaming pattern on his sweaty bald head. She paid not the slightest attention to him. He was swaying slightly, in drunken persuasion. Finally she looked up at him as if suddenly noticing him. She motioned him closer. She put her hand on the nape of his neck, pulled him down, whispered into his ear. She whispered for perhaps ten seconds. He sprang back from her. She watched him calmly. He backed into a waiter, then he turned and went back to his table. He passed quite close to us. His color looked bad, his mouth hung open. His eyes had that glassiness of someone who has been given a quick little glimpse of hell and turned into a believer.

He sat and pushed the food around his plate and then went out.

When next I looked over, she was gone.

She rapped on the inner door at precisely ten-thirty. She came in very quickly, dropped a little blue airlines bag and a big white purse onto my bed, then snugged herself into my arms, her arms locked around my waist, tightly. She was shivering, and I guessed it was half faked, half real. She kept herself pulled very firmly against me, and she whispered, "Darling, darling, darling. I'm safe now."

I gently unwound her and stepped away. "You shouldn't have packed anything."

"But I *know* that. I *didn't*! Don't be cross with your Delly. I *am* yours now, dear. What I did was make some lightning purchases, inexpensive stuff, just the essentials, dear, and that little bag to hold what I couldn't get into this purse. It's new too. He knows all my clothes. He's

like that. He's going to find everything there, my purse
and identification things and my money, what I had left.
All he'll be able to find missing is my yellow checked
jama shift, and he would have noticed that was laid out
to sleep in. It's in the blue bag, dear. He'll see I didn't
even take the darling dress I bought out of the store
wrappings, and he'll know I was upset. I even left my
dear little heart watch on the night stand. I made the
bed look as if I tried to sleep. I left the note pinned to
the pillow. I wrote it like you said, dear, about hearing
on the radio about DeeDee and Tami and realizing why
he was acting so strange. You have to lock the door
with the key, so I had to leave it unlocked. So I folded
the note and pinned it that way and wrote his name in
big letters. And I said that I just couldn't live with my
conscience any more, after what we'd done. Oh, he'll have
no doubt! So here I am, all for you, without a dime,
and just this outfit that I wouldn't be caught dead in,
usually. I bought it so I wouldn't look like me at all.
See? Short little green walking skirt, and this kind of
dumb Fauntleroy blouse and flats and little-girl stockings.
Let me show you the full effect." She hurried to her new
purse and took out a comb and seated herself in front of
the mirror. She unpinned her hair, let it fall long, and,
biting her lip, combed the pale thick weight of it. She
fashioned it into a high ponytail, fixing it so most of the
weight of it fell forward across the front of her right
shoulder. With pink lipstick she widened her mouth. She
put on a new pair of sunglasses, dainty frames and a
pixie tilt, then stood up and faced me, smiling for inspection.

"This is the way I walk off this Eyetalian sheep."

"The walk will give you away."

She trudged over to the door and back, toeing out,
slouching, swinging her arms too freely. "Will it?"

"Okay. You're eighteen. A backward eighteen."

She took the glasses off, planted herself, looked up at
me with her head cocked. "You've decided yes. I can
tell."

"On one condition."

"Anything!"

I put the sheaf of ship's stationery and my pen on the glass of the dressing table. "Sit here and write what I tell you to write."

When she had seated herself and picked up the pen, I told her to date it yesterday. "To the Police Department, Broward Beach, Florida. Dear sirs . . ."

"Hey! What are you . . ."

"Write it. You can tear it up if you want to, if you don't understand why it has to be done. You can tear it up, and then you can get out of this stateroom."

She hunched over the paper like a schoolgirl and wrote. I dictated. "I have decided to take my own life by jumping into the sea before this ship gets to Florida. I am going to give this letter to someone to mail to you."

"Just a little slower, please."

"I would rather kill myself . . . than wait and have them . . . kill me the way they did Evangeline Bellemer. Period. I think that everybody connected with this should pay for their crimes. Period. That is why I . . . am making a full confession . . . at this time. I will tell you where . . . you can find them all . . . and what we have been doing . . . for the last two years."

I waited. She finished the final words and turned and stared at me "You sure do want a hell of a lot of insurance."

"Use your head, woman. Insurance for you too. They'll break Ans Terry down in five minutes and he'll verify you jumped overboard. The cops will pick up everybody who was in on it, and there'll be nobody left to come after you if they ever did get any clue. Nobody will be looking for you, nobody from either side."

"I . . . I guess you're right. But I just hate to put it down on paper. Couldn't we do it later? You could trust me to write it all out after we're safe, dear."

"When you've written the whole thing out and signed it and I have it in my hand, addressed and stamped and sealed, then we'll talk about how much I trust you, Del."

"Jesus, you're hard, aren't you?"

"And free as a bird, and planning to stay that way. If you don't like it, go take your chances with Terry and Griff."

She spun back and snatched the pen up. "All right, all right, damn you! What next?"

"Miss Bellemer was living at . . . 8000 Cove Lane, Apartment Seven B, Quendon Beach . . . under the name of Tami Western. Period. What's Griff's name?"

"Walter Griffin."

"Walter Griffin lives at the same address in Apartment Seven C. He very probably arranged to have her killed by being struck by a car, when ordered to do so by . . . what's Mack's name?"

"Webster Macklin."

At Meyer's three solid knocks upon the stateroom door she jumped violently. I'd worked out a code with Meyer, based on several of the plausible things you can call out when somebody knocks.

"Yes?" I called. That let him know our guess was right and she had simplified things by leaving fourteen unlocked and it was safe to leave Ans his little keepsake.

"Sorry. Wrong room," he rumbled.

I kept her going. She balked now and again, such as when I demanded she put down the specifics of the most recent murder. He had been a fifty-four-year-old divorced chemist from Youngstown, Ohio, taking a vacation alone, and they had come aboard on separate tickets at separate times as Mr. and Mrs. A. B. Terry, and he had twenty-six thousand dollars in cash in a money belt, the proceeds of the sale of some bonds and the cash value of his insurance policies. Ans Terry was now wearing the money belt, and Mr. Powell Daniels was sticking out of the silted bottom somewhere west-southwest of Miami, wearing under his resort clothes an entirely different sort of belt, one of those designed for scuba diving, with every compartment snapped shut on its wafer of lead.

She explained it to me. "I'd tell him to just wander around until he was sure our luggage had been brought in. We had to come aboard separate on this one on account of crew people knowing me. He came to the cabin and I gave him a celebration drink. It would really knock them out, that stuff. Then I'd let Ans in. You could count on four or five hours before you could slap them half awake. We know where the best place is on this boat, from before. It's on the promenade deck about thirty feet forward from where the deck stops. It stops at the doors to the dining room. I guess it is about the middle of the ship. Right there there's no place above you where people can look over. There isn't any rail there or side deck on the lounge deck, and up on the sun deck there's a lifeboat in the way. It's the same on either side of the ship. You do it about three in the morning. They aren't really awake. But they sort of walk, if you hold them on both sides. We sing and ask him if he's feeling better if there's people. I go and stand at the nearest stairway and if nobody is coming, I click my tongue, and Ans picks them up like you pick up a sleepy kid, and leans out over the rail and drops them."

I dictated it back to her. Meyer had figured out the visitors' pass system perfectly.

I was curious about how so many apparently intelligent men could be gulled so readily.

"Oh, you can always tell the ones worth a try, and out of those, the ones you can get to take a real interest in you. The marrieds you brush off. Also the ones who know their way around too good. You work to get the name and home address and local address, and if they have to leave right off, that's no good. Sometimes you can go ten days without finding one worth turning in the name so Mack can get him checked out. And then a lot of times from what he found out he'd say no. Like if the guy was too important and had too much money, it would be no just as quick as if he had no chance of raising the minimum twenty thousand. When you get a go-ahead, then you keep right on with the tease, letting him get close sometimes. We all worked it just the same. You cry a lot. You say you shouldn't see him at all, that it's too dangerous. You make him meet you at hideway places at weird times. Then you confess your ex is a mental case and he's going to kill you. You tell the guy your ex has found out about him, and you make him move to another place under another name. Then you start putting out, and you butter him up by going kind of crazy and telling him it's never been like that before. After they start getting it, they'll believe any damn fool thing you tell them, and do any fool thing you ask. So you fake an attempt on your life, and you say the only way to get away is tickets under a fake name on a cruise ship and bring lots of money, because you have an old friend in Kingston or St. Thomas or somewhere the ship is going who has a remote cottage somewhere and she can fix it so the two of you can stay there under some other name indefinitely. By then, because of the way he worked the postcard bit, any relatives he has and some friends and business partners have been getting cards from him from Spokane or Toledo or Albuquerque or some place like that, and that's where they start hunting when they don't hear anything else ever. We always worked it the same exact way, but DeeDee would handle a guy different than Tami or me, and I would use a different approach than Tami. The thing is, as soon as he thinks he's going to get to spend sack time with you on a cruise ship, he hasn't got eyes for anything else. And making him believe you don't dare be with him in public makes it a lot safer. I'd always bring one suitcase full of Ans's things aboard with my stuff. How quick you could get him tuned up all the way kind of depended. One ran out on me the day before sailing. They gave me a terrible ride about that, DeeDee and Tami did. I think, all things considered, DeeDee could do the best and fastest job of nailing them down, but if in the beginning you let them think you're going to be easy to get, you spoil it. Lonely men over forty-five, they all, every one of them, have this fantastic thing about young women, and that's what you work on."

It took a long long time to flesh it all out. She became resigned to it, to the extent she did not try to drag her feet when I requested she list the fourteen. Nine was the best she could do, and she wasn't sure of two of their names. She estimated the total take of just her and Terry at close to four hundred thousand dollars.

It was after two o'clock when she said in a tired whine, "Honey, my hand is going to drop right off, honest. It's all full of cramps."

"Take a rest while I read it over."

There were fifteen pages in her unformed backhand, all the lines sloping up toward the right side of the sheets. It would give any investigator more than enough. There was little point in prying any more details out of her. Her head sagged slowly, jerked upright. She was emotionally and physically exhausted.

"Okay, Del. Just a little bit to wind it up. Ready? New paragraph. I am not going to tell Ans about this letter. I am going to leave him a note . . . saying I have killed myself. Period. I will pin it to my pillow . . . after he passes out . . . tomorrow night. Period. I am sorry about what . . . we did to those men. Period. I am glad I have written . . . this letter. Period. May God have mercy . . . on my soul. Period. Sign it, Del."

I was looking down over her shoulder as she wrote her name Adele Whitney. She hesitated. "When I was booked a few times, like in Chicago, it was my right name."

"Put that down too."

"Jane Adele Stusslund," she wrote. She dropped the pen, making a spray of ink on the paper under her signature. She stood, turning as she stood, to come up in the circle of my arms. She yawned deeply, shuddered, rested her forehead against my chin.

"Do I get a gold star, teacher?"

"Solid gold, Jane."

Her head jerked back. "Please don't call me that."

"Okay."

She yawned again. "I'm pooped something awful, darling. Would you like to undress me, maybe?"

"We'd better both rest up. Tomorrow could be rough."

Her glance was coldly inquisitive. "The times I've

been turned down you could count on one hand, friend. You gay or something?"

I slowly folded the bulky confession, stuffed it into an envelope. The *Monica D.* made a larger pitching motion, moving us both off balance, both taking a sideways step to catch ourselves, like the beginning of an improvised dance. The compartmentation creaked, and I knew we were well into New Providence Channel where we would take the sweep of the weather.

"Tomorrow I'll get you stashed in a safe place in Lauderdale. It will be four or five days before I can wind up a few things hanging fire. There'll be all the time in the world to get acquainted then, Del."

She narrowed those large brilliant eyes, cocked her head to the side. "Sure thing," she said flatly, and picked up the purse and flight bag and went into the head and banged the door shut.

When the door opened again, I had turned the stateroom lights off. I had arranged slacks, shirt and shoes in a handy pile on the floor half under my bed, on the side away from the other bed, with the thick envelope, folded once, in the hip pocket of the slacks, and my stateroom key in a side pocket. I was in my bed in underwear shorts. Through the veil of lashes I saw her stand braced in the open doorway. The heavy hair was combed long like Alice's. She wore the thing she called a jama shift. It fit loosely, blocked very little of the light behind her, had lace at the hem, throat, short sleeves, and stopped about four inches above her knees. Costume for a drowning.

The light clicked off. Darkness loudened the noises of the *Monica D.*, the buckety-swash of her rolling corkscrewing motion, the almost subsonic grumble of the marine drive downstairs, and the little phased chitters and whines that came and went as bulkhead portions picked up sympathetic resonances.

A weight came onto the bottom corner of my bed, tightening the blanket across my feet. A hand found my knee, rested there.

In a sing-song plaint, in that teeny little-girl voice

sweet as carnival candy, and while her plump little fingers massaged my blanketed knee, she said, "It's like you're leaving me out. It's like you're making all the rest of it lies and tricks, not wanting to make out with me. Words don't ever mean much. How am I supposed to feel? Jesus, Travis! Am I such a terrible pig you couldn't stand touching me? They were going to *kill* me. I don't feel safe at all. Please, honey, hold me. Make love to me. So then I'll really and truly belong to you and it will all come out fine for us. Please!"

The thing that astounded and disheartened me was to find a very real yen to take a hack at this spooky little punchboard. There had been a lot more to Vangie in both looks and substance, but she hadn't tingled a single nerve. I wanted to grab at this one. Maybe everybody at some time or another feels the strong attraction of something rotten-sweet enough to guarantee complete degradation. I wanted to pull her down and roll into that hot practiced trap which had clenched the life out of fourteen men. And there was the big shiny rationalization. It's the way to make her trust you, fella. Go right ahead, lull the broad. It'll take about nine minutes out of your life. You're a big boy. A broad is a broad is a broad, and who'll know the difference?

You will, McGee. For a long long time.

But she had to have some gesture. She had to have some assurance. So I sat up, hitched toward her, put my arms around her, tucked her face into my neck. "Everything's going to work out fine, kiddy."

Her sigh was deep and shuddering. She had shucked herself out of that jama thing, and her skin felt whisper-soft, super-heated. She clung hard and said, "Hurry, dear. Gee, I'm so ready I'm practically there already."

"No, honey. Let's wait and make it in style. I have a thing about the right time and the right place, and waiting just makes it a better blast. Why do we have to rush anything? Once we're off this nervous boat and tucked away safe, we'll spend days in bed."

"We can have that too."

I knew the quickest way to cool me off. That fat

little mouth made me squeamish. So I kissed it hard enough and long enough to creak her neck, mash the lips against her teeth, bend her rib cage. She was puffing like a little furnace when I let her loose, hoisted her off my bed, turned her and welted that behind with a pistol-crack slap.

"Hey! Ow!"

"Back to your own sack, kiddy."

She made grumbling sounds, but once she was in her own bed she giggled. "Anyways, I got proof you're not lavender, dearie."

"Try to get some sleep."

I guessed that the exhaustion of fear would catch up with her. I gave her what I hoped was enough time, then got up and dressed swiftly and silently. I leaned over her and heard slow deep buzzing snores, bee sounds that came up from the deepest part of the pool of sleep. I locked the door behind me when I left.

Meyer, squinting as he opened his door for me, looked like a sideshow bear in his awning-stripe pajamas in green, black and orange. He yawned and sighed, sat where the light was best and read Del's confession. There was no more yawning and sighing. He gave it his total attention, as if he had forgotten I was there. When he finished it, he refolded it, took it over and put it into the inside pocket of his suit jacket in the locker.

As he turned, he frowned beyond me, saying, "It is too absurd a simplification, Travis, to try to relate her actions to moralistic terms. Wickedness. Heartlessness."

"For God's sake, Meyer!"

"We can find a more appropriate answer in a book written by a woman whose name escapes me at the moment. It is called, I believe, *The I and the Not-I*. It is an extension and interpretation of one facet of Jungian theory."

"At this time in the morning?"

"She develops the concept that a frightening number of people in the world are unaware of the actual living reality of the human beings around them. It is the complete absence of empathy in action. They believe themselves to be real, of course, yet they merely lack the imagination to see that other persons are also real in the same way and on the same terms. Thus, even though they go through the obligatory social forms and personal relationships, all other people are *objects* rather than people. If all other people are objects, then there can be no psychic trauma involved in treating them as objects. That pair disposed of fourteen objects, not fourteen brothers. Their uneasiness comes not from any pity, not from any concern for the dead objects, but merely from their awareness that society frowns upon such actions."

"Meyer, please!"

"In a sense one can envy them because, unlike you and I, Travis, they cannot identify, they cannot project. We can, and so we do a lot of bleeding. We bled for a woman as wretched as Miss Bellemer. You keep remembering the look of the back of Griff's neck. This pair drifts through life without the inconvenience of such uncomfortable baggage. Interesting, isn't it, to relate this concept to conscience and to individual goals?"

"Are you through?"

"Vocalization always helps me develop such relationships."

"Meyer, *how did it go?*"

"Oh! My little visit. I slid in there like a veritable wraith. After a few moments I began to realize I could have marched through leading a fife and drum corps. At that point my heart stopped banging into my larynx and slid back down where it belongs. I selected a more effective place for our voodoo doll. The sink stopper seemed tight. I left her underwater in the sink, and fortunately it is a very deep sink. She has some buoyancy. The porous stone has absorbed enough water to hold her down. She sways with the motion of the ship. An eerie effect. Drunks often have to make a bathroom journey in the small hours. I left the bathroom light on for the fellow. When you are beginning to emerge into hangover, the world is slightly hallucinatory. It might take him quite some time to identify the real and the unreal."

"Remind me not to wake you up at this time of day. You are so ornate you give me a headache. I call your attention to where the Powell Daniels money is at the moment."

"Around Terry's middle. So?"

"If we don't want him making a successful run for it, I better take the wings off his heels."

He glanced at his watch. "It's after four. The depressant effects are diminishing. He's had perhaps seven hours. I don't think the risk is justified, Travis. He's an exceptionally brawny brute. Why don't you just leave well enough alone?"

"I'm going to give it a try."

Shrewd eyes studied me. "I find the compulsion odd. Your normal cheer has soured. Could it be possible the little pig required the bargain be sealed, in her manner?"

"Get off my back, Meyer."

"And so the derring-do is a penance, a reaffirmation of the real identity of the McGee, a symbolic scrubbing of the soiled escutcheon."

"Do you really think I cut myself a slice of *that*?"

"Dear boy, if I thought so, I wouldn't be making such a dull joke about it."

"Then be advised I came damned close."

His eyes went round. "Actually?"

"Seems I'm less fastidious than I thought. So maybe there is a little flavor of escutcheon-scrubbing in the air after all."

"The wish is not the deed, except to apologists. You didn't follow through. And, if you had, after all she is young, pneumatic, lubricious, and no doubt highly competent. Also, any parent will tell you that if you dress a child in his best and send him out to play, he will find the deepest, sloppiest mud puddle in town and stomp around in it, perfectly aware of the whomping he'll get when he goes home. There is sometimes a hypnotic deliciousness about dirt."

I grinned at him. "I need you around more often, sire. Okay. All straight on the rest of your duties?"

"Completely. And be very careful with that fellow."

I climbed the aft ladderways to the lounge deck and stood at the fantail rail. We were quartering into a north-west wind. The ship grunted and chugged its way across a black and lumpy sea, leaving in the churned wake a faint green-white of phosphorescence.

I debated going after the mild authoritative weight of the Bodyguard. But I didn't want to risk awakening her. And didn't want to admit to myself there was any chance I couldn't handle a sleeping drunk no matter how many layers of muscle he wore.

THIRTEEN

I CLOSED the door of Stateroom Fourteen without a sound, and stood for a long time, waiting for my eyes to adjust to the slight glow in the room which came from the yellow crack of light shining out from under the door of the head.

At last I could see the shapes emerge, the silent length of him in the far bed, the vague bulks of the furniture, even the oblong of the note pinned to the pillow of the empty bed. I moved to the porthole and worked the curtains aside so that a nearby deck light increased the inner illumination. From there I could look down upon him, and hear the slow rasp of his breathing. He was on his left side, tilting toward the prone position, hands wedged under his pillow, right leg bent, the knee bracing him.

I moved around behind him. The covers were halfway to his waist. I reached across him with my right hand, and with both hands I carefully picked up the coverings and turned them slowly down until when I doubled them back, the folded edge was below his waist. He slept in a pajama top. I nipped the loose edge of it and folded it upward. Around the lean fitness of Mr. Body's waist was the dark band of the moneybelt, perhaps four inches wide. It was too dark to see how it fastened. It looked as if it could be one of those types made of GI fabric which have two straps and two buckles in front, one above the other.

With infinite care I ran my fingertips around him,

lightly brushing the fabric of the belt. In the front, right in the middle of him, I felt the little metal edges of the buckles, the strap tongues. His belly lifted and fell with his breathing, and closing my eyes so as to focus my whole perception on touch, I made certain that I knew just how they were fastened. One at a time I worked each strap out of the leather loop. The next step was more difficult, the problem of pulling the straps through the first metal part of the buckles. There was a slight loosening at the bottom of each exhalation. I pulled gently each time he exhaled, and gained perhaps a quarter inch each time. It took a half dozen exhalations to release each strap. His sweat and breath smelled rich with booze. Then, all that held the belt were the little metal prongs through the strap holes. I pulled on the strap of the bottom one first. Each time he exhaled, I risked a slightly increased pressure. Then, in my fingertips, I felt the little pop as the buckle was freed. I knew how I would work it. Get the other one open, then gently lay the belt open so that it was held by the weight of him. After that, stealth would be the greater risk. I would merely get a good grip on it, snatch it violently out from under him and be out the door before he could paw the cobwebs out of his eyes, taking the off chance of not meeting a member of the ship's company in the corridor.

Perhaps I was thinking more of the final steps than the final buckle. Or I had to tug harder at it. He grunted, rolled toward me, brought a hand down quickly, so quickly his fingertips brushed the back of my hand before I could get it away.

I heard his hand patting at the buckles. He sat up quickly. "Bitch!" he said. "You damn bitch! What the hell are you doing?"

As I saw him lean to reach toward the light switch, I clenched my hands together, chopped down hard at the exposed side of his throat. But in the darkness I hit too far back, and my fists rebounded off the great rubbery bulk of the trapezius muscle, and he disconcerted me with the speed with which he came lunging off the bed, shoulder slamming into my chest, big arms clamping and locking around me as he drove me back onto her empty bed. I felt my whole rib cage bending, and he had the sense to keep his face tucked against me so I couldn't get at his eyes. He grunted with effort and I felt blackness moving in behind my eyes. I chopped at the nape of his neck with my fist, but I couldn't get enough force into the awkward blows. I found an ear, wadded it small, and tried twisting it off, but the pain merely increased his power. Then, knowing there was only one chance left, I got my thumb under the corner of his jaw, fingers clamped for leverage around the back of the bull neck, and with waning strength, dug that thumb in as deeply as I could. He wheezed, and the pressure slackened enough for me to fill my lungs, pushing the darkness back. Suddenly he released me, yanked his hand back and tried a clubbing punch to the face, misjudged the distance, hit me squarely in the throat. The pain galvanized me into a leaping spasm that carried us both off the bed and down onto the floor between the beds. My throat felt full of broken gravel. He was underneath. I picked his head up by the ears and banged it down as hard as I could, twice. Then he wormed to the side, rocked up onto his shoulders, clamped me diagonally across the chest with bare legs as hard as marble, and if he'd had one more half second to bear down, that would have ended it. But I made a frantic grab at his crotch. He gave a whistling scream, flopped and floundered away, got hold of my fingers, loosened my grip, pulled himself loose, scrambled up before I could and, as I was coming up, kicked me solidly and squarely on the point of the chin with the hard front pad of his right foot. I spilled over onto my back, perfectly conscious, but absolutely unable to move a finger or even blink my eyes or move my tongue to the other side of my mouth.

I lay there thinking with a great coldness that the most probable finish of our little rumble would be for him to lift a bare foot high, and stamp it down onto my throat. And the rail was the other side of the other door, just ten feet across the dark weather deck. "To him, you are just an object," Meyer said in a lecturer's tone.

My dead head rolled from side to side as the ship rolled. When it rolled toward him, I could see him. He sat on the edge of his bed, head between his knees, making soft crooning noises.

He got up and with a painful deliberation, he edged by me, doubled over, and went to the door of the head and opened it. I moved a finger, a whole hand. I bent my right knee. I pushed myself over onto my face, got my hands against the floor, lifted the full eighty tons of myself up onto hands and knees, reached and caught the footboard of her bed, climbed up onto my macaroni legs. I turned and looked into the head. He stood, bent over, in front of the sink. He cuddled himself with one hand, and in the other he held the dripping doll, the cinderblock swinging.

His mouth kept opening and closing, but I could not hear a sound. Life was running back into my muscles, like Popeye after the great hunk of canned spinach drops down his throat. He seemed frozen there, unaware of me, unaware of anything. I went to the doorway. The jaw shelf was turned just right, at the height of the middle of my chest, and three feet away. I took a hand towel from the rack, wrapped my right fist tightly, screwed my heels into the floor and started it with a pivot of hips and back, the fist moving ten inches to the impact point, and following through a good long yard, my knuckles almost brushing the floor. He moved a half step to the side, fell so loosely his forehead bounced when it hit the tile. I found the moneybelt half under her bed. The second strap had torn loose.

When I was ready to leave, I took a final look around. I had put him back into his bed, in the position I had found him. The breathing sounded the same. The single strap held the moneybelt safely and snugly around my middle, under my shirt. I had both parts of the doll in my hand. When the dark head had broken off, it had rolled into a corner, but when I was hunting for it, the movement of the ship brought it rolling back out to meet me. I had let the water out of the sink.

And he would not know what parts of it were real.

After the early honking and bell ringing, shouts in the corridors, hasty rappings on the stateroom door, announcements to get all baggage into the corridors as quickly as possible, I dressed quickly. She had not moved a muscle, lay in a spill of cream hair, fatty little lips agape, eyes smudged with weariness.

According to his little placard, the room steward was named Arturo Taliapeloleoni.

I moved him back into a corner of his little office. *"Scusi,"* I said. "I wish to ask you to help me with something of the greatest importance, *per favore.*"

The blow in the throat had given my voice an unmistakably conspiratorial quality. It made him look apprehensive. "Ah?" he said.

"I am in *numero sei.* Here is a token of importance."

He accepted it too casually, thinking it a ten. Then he saw the second zero and the color went out of his face, surged back pinkly. "If it is *anything* I can do, *Signore.*" The bill had flicked out of sight.

"I bought passage alone. But now there is a lady in my stateroom. She is from other quarters aboard. It is of the greatest importance that she and I be permitted to remain aboard until midmorning."

"That would be impossible, truly!"

"Many things can be arranged. Indeed, they *must* be arranged. Or it is possible that as she walks out of the customs building her husband might shoot her right there, in front of your passengers. He is a violent man. Others could be hurt. It would not be good for the company."

Even his lips were pale. "It would be very bad. But there is the question of the luggage inspection, no?"

"Her luggage will be taken off by someone. Mine will be taken off by someone else, a friend. It will go through customs and be taken away."

"But if two passengers are missing?"

"The one who counts them could be told of the necessity for this arrangement." I dipped my fingertips into my shirt pocket and extracted the other two bills, a fifty and a twenty. I gave him the fifty. "This could purchase some small cooperation in the counting?"

"It is possible."

I gave him the twenty. "And this, of course, is for yourself and the room maid."

"The cleaning and the fumigation starts. From stateroom to stateroom."

"Does not a man of your position have a sign he can place upon both doors of *numero sei,* that it is to be skipped until certain other work is accomplished? After all, you do not sail for the homeland until Friday, I understand."

"It is very difficult, but. . . ."

"How many chances in one lifetime does a man have to save the life of a beautiful woman?"

He straightened, lifted his chin. "It will be done!"

"You have great understanding."

When I went back to the room, she had still not stirred. I sorted out the minimum essentials she would need. Her white purse would hold them readily. I put the yellow and white checked pajama shift in the flight bag, squashed the bag flat enough to go into my bag, and, locking the door behind me again, toted it down to Meyer's hovel.

"Have you got a cold?" he asked.

I dropped the bag in the corridor outside the door. His was there. Both were tagged. They'd both end up on the M table at customs inspection. I pulled the door shut, pulled my shirt loose, unstrapped the money belt.

He put it on, and I helped him fasten it with the aid of two pieces of cord to bridge the six or seven inch gap between the ends of the straps and the buckles.

"Just in case," I said, "anything goes wrong about getting off this bucket. In case somebody thinks it's a smuggler's cute trick."

He adjusted his shirt, patted his belly. "This is a damned poor way for an economist to handle money."

"Just while we're standing here, sure, it could have been earning twenty-two cents. Your next step is to act like a hostile lady in a supermarket."

"If I am not the first off, McGee, I shall be no further back than third place."

"I flipped your art work over the side. Sorry."

"And the fellow with it?"

"No. He'll wonder how much of it he dreamed. He never saw my face. But he'll know it wasn't Del who roughed him. He got his look at the doll. It put him into shock. I deepened it a little and tucked him into the beddy-bye. The steward is bribed. The pig buzzes like a bee, and we are a pair of unmitigated, revolving, reprehensible sons of bitches."

"Revolving?"

"No matter from which direction the object is viewed." I opened the door. "Best of luck."

When I got back, notices were taped to both of the stateroom doors, in an ornate Italianate script. I went in and pushed the inside lock. Her bed was empty, the bathroom door half open, water running.

I tapped on the door.

"Darling?"

"It's all fixed."

"Come in, dear."

I went in. The two small bulbs made a dingy light in the small bathroom. She was sitting in the deep narrow little tub, using the shower head off the bracket, taking a sit-down shower. Her hair, gathered together and pinned at the nape of her neck, spilled down her back. Her face was scrubbed clean, a line of suds drying along her jaw. She smiled up at me, a softness in the huge green eyes.

"Morning, lover," she said.

"Did you hear me say that I. . . ."

"Sure. I knew you'd fix it." She soaped the washcloth, handed it to me and said, "Do my back, huh?" She reached and got her hair and piled it up on her head, held it there and leaned forward, resting her forehead against her round wet knees.

"There's women aboard, honest to Betsy, they're a yard at least across the can, and I just barely fit into this crazy tub. I bet they're always having to bring a gang of little wops into these cans and yank them loose. Gee, I kept hearing all the noise going on and dropping right back off to sleep. Done, darling? Thanks. Look, take this shower thing and rinse the suds off my back. Then dry me so I can let go of my hair. Honest, my hair is so thick and heavy, if it gets wet it doesn't dry for hours."

When I had finished the requests, she shook her hair back, rinsed the washcloth, wrung it out, soaped it again and held it out to me, saying, "You did so good on the back, you get to wash the front too."

"No time for games, kiddy. Hurry it up."

"Why are you cross? Did you catch a cold? Your voice is husky. Can't you sit over there and talk to me?"

"I'm not cross, but I am nervous. If my arrangements don't work, I'd rather have you dressed and on your feet if some ship's officers or customs people come hammering at the door."

"All right, dear," she said, unexpectedly humble and obedient.

It was quarter to eight, and I went out, spotted the channel buoy and estimated we'd be tied up in thirty minutes. I came across Arturo Taliapeloleoni, gave him a breakfast order and let him make another bill disappear. He brought it ten minutes later. I hustled her into the bathroom and took the tray from him at the door while he tried to peer around me without seeming to do so. With a conspirator's grimace, he left.

She squeaked with delight at the breakfast tray, especially at the carafe of brandy I'd ordered for the coffee. After she sat down and had taken the first sip of the iced juice, she tilted her head to the side and said, "Hey, we're slowing down now."

"Coming in past the breakwater now."

"When will we get off, darling?"

"Eleven, I guess. I want to get up there in a few minutes and make sure Terry gets off without creating any disturbance."

"He'll creep off like a rabbit, believe me. Why worry about him?"

"Also, I want to see if there are any cops waiting for the two of you. If this thing is coming apart, they might

have more than you know. I can watch and see if anybody takes him when he gets off. That might change
the whole picture."

She stopped chewing and through a wad of sweet roll
said, "Howf it change if?"

"If they ask the ship's officers about you, the room
steward is going to put two and two together and imme-
diately turn chicken."

She began chewing again, slowly. "Hell, they couldn't
get that close to it so soon. No." She winked at me. "But
they'll sure get close fast when they get the confession.
Hey, what'd you do with it?"

"Printed the address on it, put the stamps on it, and
gave it to my friend to mail when he gets ashore."

"Honey, I think we should have mailed it. What if he
gets curious? I'd be curious about a letter addressed to the
cops."

"I make the decisions. And what do you do?"

"I . . . I do what you say. Okay, darling. That's the way
it will be. That's the way I want it, too. You're the boss
man."

I gulped the second half of my cup of coffee, warned
her about not answering any knock, relocked the door
from the outside. I went down to the promenade deck.
They were easing the starboard up to the big wharf. There
were about a hundred people in their bright clothing and
sunbrown skin standing behind the chest-high hurricane
fencing in the morning sunshine, awaiting the passengers
and crew of the last cruise of the season of the *Monica D.*
They were waving. I could hear the yelps of greeting.
Cars glittered in the parking area. The deck crew heaved
the big hawsers, and the shore hands dropped the loops
over the big iron bollards. The deck winches groaned
and took the slack and slowly snubbed the length and
weight of her against the wharf. Her deep rumbling of the
main engines stopped, leaving the thinner sound of her
generators supplying the shoreside ship's services. Two
gangplanks were swung up and latched, and as the ship's
captain and two of his officers went down the gangplank
in spotless whites, carrying small handbags and brief-

cases, the PA system aboard blared that all debarking passengers should gather on the promenade deck at the amidships gangplank prepared to leave the ship as soon as all the luggage was off.

I moved aft to a place where I could see the ship's end of the passenger gangplank, and I saw Meyer there, belly firm against the rail, first in line. He did not see me. He looked very resolute. The cargo hatch in the lower hull had been opened, and the gravity roller conveyor set in place. Baggage was coming down and the porters were filling the first big hand truck. They would roll it into the shed and begin filling the next one, while in the customs shed other porters would hustle it, according to alphabetical name of the passenger on the tag, to the proper customs section. One out of every three pieces coming off seemed to be one of the straw liquor baskets. The passengers were lined up, clutching customs declarations and proof of vaccination, the ones wedged near the rail peering over and trying to identify their own pieces of luggage. The shoreside PA system began to wham out a series of marches, the speakers so overloaded much of it was just an overlapping resonant blur. A few favored passengers were paged and directed to go forward to the other gangplank. They were the ones with a little political leverage. They had to walk down the wide wharf corridor between the wire fence and the side of the ship, past their fellow passengers whose impatience to get off was further stimulated by this demonstration of privilege. The one-class ship in the last minutes of the cruise had become a two-class ship, and the favored dozen walked a little stiffly under the pleasant burden of importance, chatting together with excess animation. In the shed they would get a head start on the inspection.

Suddenly I saw Meyer among them. His name had not been called. He walked like the king of all the bears, looking up at the ship, searching me out. Spotting me, he made a single airy little gesture, a prince of the blood flipping a florin to the humble peasant. And if he ran into any special curiosity inside the doors of the shed, I could guess exactly how he would handle it, with cold professorial gaze, great pomposity, excluding any possibility that Herr Doktor Professor Meyer could be given anything but the most privileged treatment.

I then saw him searching among the visitors behind the wire, as I was, to spot Merrimay Lane, our imitation Vangie. I believe he saw her just as I did, standing in too dense a clot of people, and he veered over to her, moved her along. They walked on either side of the wire fence until she had reached an open space. He paused and said a few more words to her, then hastened to catch up with the rest of the privileged ones, matching his quick stride to the blare of *Stars and Stripes Forever.*

I had not been able to spot Ans Terry, and I began to have worrisome visions of him in his bed exactly as I had left him, the blood ball in his brain slowly suppressing the automata of lungs and heart. His head had bounced pretty well. And even with the towel, I had knuckles sufficiently puffed to create four temporary dimples. The brain jelly bounces around inside the shell and the skull, sometimes tears readily. Lesser damage can leave the customer comatose for seven hours, seven weeks or seven years.

As my concern grew, I finally went hurrying back up to the lounge deck. Fourteen was wide open, and two maids were in there stripping the beds, chirping at each other in the cheery fluidities of Italian. It was a noticeably happy crew. The last cargo of sunburn had been trucked around the islands, the last sheaf of tips safetypinned to the underpants, and Friday they'd be homeward bound with, at the end of the voyage, two weeks with the family while the *Monica D.* was freshened up in one of the company docks at Naples in preparation for the first July cruise to Mediterranean ports.

Before going down again, I went to the rail, leaned out and looked upward and saw, about twenty feet forward of where I stood, Ans Terry leaning on the starboard rail of the sun deck.

There were other people up there too, couples spaced at wide intervals along the rail. These were the relaxed ones, who saw no point in jamming themselves into the throng on the lower deck. When the herd began to thunder off, they would drift on down and saunter off. They are the same people who keep their seats in airplanes while the sheep-like clog the aisle waiting for the doors to be opened. When the aisle is clear, they get up, gather their possessions, and quite often manage to get their luggage first and catch the first cab.

I went on up. I took a position about ten feet aft of Terry. His long sallow grooved face looked empty. His body was unnaturally motionless. I could see a little purple knot on his forehead, half of a grape. Trying to imagine what was going on in his mind, I had a sudden vivid memory of going to a small zoo when I was a kid, and being fascinated by the ceaseless, purposeless pacing of a polar bear. He went back and forth across the front of his cage. Six strides each way, shifting weight and direction exactly the same way as he made each turn. That could be very much like what Ans Terry's brain was doing. He could not know Vangie had escaped her watery grave. Only he and Macklin knew where she'd been dropped and how she had been weighted. But there had been the reality of the drowned doll in his hand, looking like Vangie. Now Del had written a farewell note that made little sense and had gone over the side. And somebody had come in in darkness and taken the money. His mind would be pacing back and forth, six strides, always the same, trying to find some relationship between these things.

He was not looking down. He was staring straight out, at nothing. I looked down and saw Merrimay in that open place along the fence. She stood with one hand holding the pipe that ran along the top of the chest-high fence. Her head was tilted back and she was looking up at me. I turned a little away from Ans Terry, and pointed my shielded right hand at him, three poking gestures. She nodded. She was wearing dark glasses.

A march ended. Into the electronic scratchiness between bands she yelled up at us. "Ans! Hey, Ans!"

His body tightened and he stared down. The next march started. I saw him find her and stare at her. She waved, pulled the glasses off, stood in Vangie's exaggeratedly hipshot way, and stared right up at him with Vangie's wide mocking grin.

He stared down at her, leaning forward further, his big hard yellowish hands clamping the rail. His mouth hung open. I looked down at her. She kissed the palm of her hand, blew the kiss upward. He made a sound half gag and half cough, and when I looked back toward him, I saw a shine of spittle on his chin, a wet strand swinging.

Suddenly he whirled and sprinted for the stairway. A couple was just turning away from the rail, middle-aged, quite smartly dressed. Terry did not change stride or direction. He dropped his shoulder slightly and plunged through the six-inch space between them. The man was whirled and slammed into the rail, and caught the rail and kept from falling. The small woman plunged off at an angle, arms flailing for balance, legs running to try to catch up, but she leaned further and further forward, and I was running as fast as I could to try to catch her. It was all slow motion. She pitched headlong into a stack of folded deck chairs, twisting the precision of the stack, tumbled loosely onto her back, rolling slack, the blood welling quickly through the multiple lacerations. I got a glimpse of her as I veered to follow Terry, and behind me I heard her husband yelling in a cracked voice of terror, anger and outrage, "Help! Help!" Martial music blurred and smothered his appeal. As I reached the deck below I saw Terry just disappearing down the next ladderway to the main deck. Behind him a fat man sat on the deck, bawling indignations. And as I tried to go around him, with an unexpected agility he extended a foot and hooked my ankle. I slapped both hands smartly on the deck, tucked my shoulder under and rolled, came up onto my feet, took three jolting backward steps and sat down solidly, facing the fat man. The two of us got up like mirror images of each other.

"Stop all the goddamn running!" he yelled. "Busted a whole pocketful of cigars."

"I was trying to stop *him* from running."

"One of you is more than enough, buddy. Take your

time. Everybody will get to get off. There's too much running."

I heard a hoarse excitement of shouts, went quickly to the rail, and stared down and saw Ans Terry coming down the gravity conveyor, sitting up, riding backward, clubbing with his fist at the burly deck hand who had hold of one ankle. The punishment knocked the man loose, and Terry grabbed the low stationary side rail which kept the luggage from falling off, swung his legs over, hung, dropped lightly to the concrete wharf, spun and headed directly toward the place where Merrimay stood behind the wire. The Bodyguard chunked solidly into the meat of my hand, and I used my left forearm and the rail as a brace and squatted to aim at him, too aware of the decreasing accuracy of the short barrel at such an increasing distance, remembering it would throw high at the downward angle, and if I aimed at the small of his back I should hit the target area of the big back and, with my luck, knock him down. The blind violent beast-like urgency to get to the dead Vangie could have only one interpretation, a necessity to finish it again, regardless of consequence.

But an agile and wiry porter came from the side and sprang onto that broad back, locking his arms around Terry's throat. He staggered under the additional weight, kept going more slowly. A dock guard trotted in to intercept him, and whaled him mightily across the belly with his billy club, an approach that reduces ninety-nine out of a hundred men to the immediate level of ferocity of an Easter bunny. But he was whamming a triple layer of muscles trained to the hardness of interwoven cordovan. Terry grasped the club, stopped, planted his heels, made a swinging motion like a hammer throw. The guard had the thong around his wrist. Somebody had shut off the music. I heard the brisk snap of bone as the guard went rolling across the cement. While stopped, Terry evidently decided to remove the minor annoyance on his back. He broke the hold on his throat, took the man's wrists, bent abruptly forward, a deep strong bow, a yanking leverage of the arms which sent the little brave one through the air to sprong into the wire mesh fifteen feet away and rebound. All the people had backed away from the fence. Merrimay, to my absolute and total astonishment, stood her ground, the knowing smile in place.

As I started to aim, the burly chap who'd been knocked loose on the conveyor and had ridden it all the way down, got to Terry, clapped a hand on a bull shoulder, spun him and hit him with great enthusiasm, squarely in the mouth. The people aboard and ashore were strangely silent. I could hear some little kids crying. Men were converging on the action with varying degrees of haste and caution. Terry hooked the burly optimist in the middle, doubling him into slow-motion collapse. A guard bounced a billy club off the sculptured blond curls. Two baggage handlers hit him high and low. Two hands from the ship were competing to hit him in the face. And then the cautious ones came diving in. Some went staggering back, rubber-legged. One went down and started making unsuccessful efforts to get up. They bore Terry down, but he came floundering halfway up, and a man screamed and went waddling away, clasping himself. Terry was erect for a moment more, and somebody had snatched off the hairpiece. His skull glistened, and I heard the tock when the club rapped it. He melted down from view, and turmoil ended. They began getting off him, moving back, fingering their faces and looking at their hands for blood. A dock guard bent over Terry, gathered the limp arms behind him, clicked handcuffs on him. Overhead, on the boat deck, the same cracked voice was yelling, "Get a doctor! Quick! Get a doctor!"

The fat man stood beside me. He was looking down at the snubbed thirty-eight still in my hand. I shoved it down into the holster until it clicked in place. The fat man said, "I don't know anything about anything, and I got terrible eyesight." He moved away from me, walking briskly.

Everybody aboard and ashore had suddenly become noisy, telling each other what they had seen. And, of course, everybody had seen something quite different. The last of the casualties were up on their feet, some of them leaning on friends. Terry began rolling from side to side, and they plucked him up and stood him on his feet, trickles of blood coming from fresh welts on the hairless skull. He went along, docile, one holding each arm. After about ten steps he suddenly began leaping, writhing and kicking, and began a terrible, spine-chilling, open-jawed howling. "Haaooo Haaooo Haoooo." It stilled the crowd sounds. He tore loose from one man. The other was hanging on and being spun around. A third trotted up, timed the spinning, and clopped him on the skull again. Terry went down to his knees. They yanked him up and led him away to some structure beyond the customs shed. He stumbled along, head bowed and wobbling from side to side. The crowd noise had started up again. A dock guard walked to the blond hairpiece, bent over it, stared curiously at it. He reached to pick it up, pulled his hand back, wiped the hand on his thigh. It gave the crowd the release of laughter, semi-hysterical. The guard took the billy club and scooped it up, holding it at arm's length, balanced atop the club. He acknowledged laughter and applause with a little bow toward the ship, then toward the fence, and marched off just as, with the timing only accident can achieve, the PA system began the *Colonel Bogie March*.

I looked at Merrimay. She looked up at me, slipped the glasses back on, made a little shrug of query, palms extended. I made a circle of thumb and forefinger, and she nodded and turned and began walking to the place where it had been agreed Meyer would meet her as soon as he had cleared through customs. The last of the baggage was being trundled in. The chain was dropped and the herd started down the gangplank in their cruise hats and salt water burn. I went quickly back to Stateroom six. It was nine o'clock.

She looked up as I came in, all the questions written on her face.

"No sweat," I said. "He got off okay. No reception committee."

"That's what I figured. Sweetheart, what was all the roaring going on out there?"

"Somebody got off drunk. A drunk dropping parcels, picking up two and dropping three more, that's real comedy."

The big pot had kept the coffee reasonably hot. Arturo had provided a generous little flagon of brandy, and she had lowered the level of it an inch or so. I had the inner trembles from thinking of how narrowly Terry had missed getting his hands on Merrimay, so I laced mine generously.

From time to time we heard loud happy Italian passing by in the corridor and on deck. The cleanup squads. She had wiped her mouth clean of the pinkness.

She turned my wrist and looked at my watch. "I'm lost without my little heart watch. I keep looking at my empty wrist all the time. It kept wonderful time. I got it at a discount place. Ninety bucks. It retails for a hundred and seventy-five." She leaned and stroked my arm, widened her big green eyes at me. "Gee, what a break you're getting, huh? Just me in these dumpy clothes, and not even a penny in my purse for luck. Poor McGee. And I've got whole racks and drawers full of the most darling clothes, and anyway forty pairs of shoes—that's my vice, buying shoes—and more perfume than a store, and I can't go near it. I suppose Ans'll sell it. Or go try to recruit a girl my size. Oh, I forgot for a minute. You said they'll probably knock him off too, and Frankie Loyal." She closed her eyes, shook her head, tapped her temple with a stubby forefinger. "I must be losing my *mind!* When the cops get that letter, nobody is going to have time to do anything. It's weird, you know, thinking I'll be the only one that got away. Just on account of you're so terribly smart, T . . . T. . . . Darling, would you forgive me? It's kind of insulting, I know, but you told me your front name and I know it starts with a T, but I can't seem to remember it."

"Travis. Trav."

"Okay, I'll never forget again. Travis like travel. Because we're going to travel, baby. Far and wide. Do you know how good for you I'm going to be? You don't even know the half yet. What kind of a place do you hide me out in in Lauderdale? Cute, maybe? I don't really care if it's a shack or a cellar or something. You know something, honey? I feel like a kid when summer vacation starts. I got to have a new name. But you have to like it or I won't use it. I was thinking of one. I want to see if you like it. What I was thinking, the first name should have like the same sound I'm used to. You know, so I'll answer. So I thought Nel. There aren't many Nels around, and it is kinda quainty. Then for a last name I thought of the store names along Bay Street because we met there. And how about one of those with a hyphen in the middle? That hyphen stuff has always churned me up. So tell me if you like this. Miss Nel Cole-Thompson."

"Just great," I said. I divided the last of the coffee. She wanted just a touch of brandy and I took the rest.

She came around behind me, and dug her fingers into the muscles near the nape of my neck. "Trav, dear, you're just all knotted up. It's all this tension that's making you seem so cross. Let your head hang loose. Breathe deep and let's see." She struggled diligently, digging and prodding and rubbing.

"No use," she said finally. She came around me, slid onto my lap, arm around my neck. She kissed my ear, huffed a little blast of warm breath into it. "What we're going to do, we got plenty of time. Del . . . I mean Nel is going to relax you her way. All you do, is you just lie down and close your eyes tight."

"Too much chance of Arturo not being able to make his arrangements stick."

She shrugged, sighed, got up. "Okay. But when we get where we're going, sweetheart, we're going to have us what they call acres of afternoon, and you can believe it. You're going to get so relaxed you won't know or care who you are any more. Me too."

She paced for a little while, looked at my watch again, then curled up on the bed, propped on the pillows, and prattled on and on about her childhood in Austin, Minnesota.

As I listened, I could not help relating her to the theory Meyer had propounded in the small hours. She could blithely accept the abrupt disappearance of Ans Terry from her life forever after seven years of his ownership because she was the "I" and Ans was the "Not-I", hence merely an object, and when any object lost its utility to the "I", it could be discarded without a backward glance. Of late he had lost his utility as a pleasure-object, and I had moved in to fill the void. The fourteen victims were forgotten the moment she felt assured she would escape punishment. Her tears for Vangie had also been without meaning, a concession to the tradition of mourning a friend, because Vangie too had been an object, something that had hung on a wall of one of the rooms of her life, and were life to take her back into that room, she would miss Vangie the way one might miss a mirror that had always hung in a certain spot. If one became associated with an object that could inflict pain when displeased, one merely took the precaution of pleasing the object.

Probably she thought she was treating me in a very special way by telling me the details of her childhood, girlhood, life with Ans Terry. The things she remembered were empty and trivial. The shallowness of her mind gave her a spurious flavor of innocence.

She had taken no part in the direction of her life. She had let life happen to her, and her pleasure was in her clothes, in her figure, in pleasing and being admired by men, in enjoying sex, in changing her hairdo.

She was twenty-three. Any pattern of life she had drifted into would have left her essentially the same, with the same interests and the same emptinesses.

At last I told her it was time we were leaving. She pinked her mouth again, put the dark glasses on, snapped her purse shut and said, "Boy, I was really getting fed with these cruises."

I left her there and took a look and found the dockside empty. I went back and got her and took her down the gangplank. A gate in the wire fence had been left ajar. We went through and she stood in the shade of the customs shed while I phoned for a taxi. We had a five-minute wait.

When we walked through the sunlight to the open door of the cab, she gave me an assured little smile and a hearty swinging thud with a healthy hip.

FOURTEEN

THE DRIVER, following my directions, drove out of the port area onto Route One and turned left. After four blocks, I said, "Driver, I've got some phone calls to make. Would you please pull into that shopping center ahead on your right and park as close as you can to the drugstore."

He found a slot at the very end of the herringbone pattern, the closest parking area to the drugstore. The cab was airconditioned.

I patted her on the leg and said, "Just hold still a while, honey. There are some things I have to take care of, a few little arrangements to make. For us. Shouldn't be more than five minutes or so."

"Okay, honey," she said.

I reached, tapped the driver on the shoulder, put a five in his hand. "In case you get restless," I said.

"In the rain, five o'clock traffic, a fare has to make the airport in four minutes, I get restless, buddy. Otherwise, never."

I whispered in Del's ear. "Try to be inconspicuous. Just in case."

"Anything you say, that I do."

They had expanded the shopping center by opening an entire new area behind it, on the side street. Some of the shops had merely doubled their area and taken another store front on the new side. The drugstore was one. Meyer and Merrimay were in the last booth in the row opposite the counter. She was back to blonde, the wig stowed away, the transparent film peeled from the flesh beside her eyes so that their contour was back to normal. Her mouth was redrawn to her own taste. And somewhere she had changed to a short-sleeved red and white striped blouse, a split red skirt. They both looked and acted very edgy.

"How close could he park?" Meyer asked.

"Smack dab in front."

"Good!"

She stood up, showed us the dime in her outstretched hand. "It had better be the same girlish voice as before, don't you think?"

"Yes indeed," Meyer said. She hurried off toward the booths. "There is a very dandy girl. She thought of a good way to get the confession to them. She kept her Vangie suit on, and her Vangie hair, and she stopped a kid a half block from the station and gave him a buck to hustle it to the homicide people."

"When did she phone back?"

"Ten-thirty. She got right through to the top brass. They admitted right off it was a very interesting document, and a copy had already been rushed up to Broward Beach. Then she asked them if they'd like to lay their hands on the girl who wrote it. She'd changed her mind about killing herself. She was trying to get out of the area. She said she could hear them drooling. They tried to stall her, keep her on the line. She told them to have a prowl car waiting six blocks north of here, in the Howard Johnson parking lot, and hung up."

Merrimay came back to the booth and said, "We better take off, don't you think?"

We walked into the new area. She had her car, a little white Corvair hardtop. She handed me the keys. Meyer clambered into the back seat.

As I backed out of the parking slot, I said, "Morbid curiosity, anyone?"

"Might as well see the end of it," Meyer said.

I circled the block, drifted into the lot on the other side, went up an aisle two parked rows away, turned into an empty slot. Through the tilted back window of the cab we could see her pale head.

The patrol car came in with a deft swiftness, stopped with a small yelp of tires directly behind the cab, blocking it there. The blinker light was revolving, bright even in sunlight. A pair in pale blue piled out with guns in hand. Shoppers stopped and gawked.

The cab door popped open and Del sprang out and took off between the parked cars, running diagonally away from us. The short green skirt did not impede her, and she ran well on those long legs. Yelling at her to stop, the police ran after her. One followed her between the cars. The other sprinted down the aisle to circle her and cut her off. For a time our vision of the chase was obscured, and then we could see them catch her in an open space. She tried to flail them with the white purse and one snatched it away. She kicked at them but one got behind her and grabbed her around the middle, pinning her arms, and lifted her off her feet. The other one snapped a cuff onto her right wrist, snapped the other onto his own left wrist. Then she stood docile, head lowered. A crowd was gathering. The cop tugged at her and she came along with him, through the circle of people. She did not look up. The cab driver was standing with his hands on his hips. Another patrol car had arrived. I had not seen it appear. Other cops were talking to him and I saw him shrug and point at the drugstore. Two of them marched in with him, hoping no doubt to nail me in a phone booth.

They were slipping her into the rear seat of the first patrol car. I said an exceptionally ugly word with an exceptionally ugly emphasis, and backed out and drove to the highway, and turned north, toward the broad boulevard which would take us over to Bahia Mar.

After a block of silence I said to Merrimay in the bucket seat beside me, "Excuse the language."

"I think we may have said it simultaneously, Travis."

"All three of us," Meyer said.

"Merrimay," I asked, "how come you just stood there when Terry was coming at you?"

"I guess the cameras were rolling, and when you have all those extras in one scene, you don't want to run into a lot of retakes. I guess it just wasn't real to me, somehow. I was Vangie, and he had tried to kill me, and the instant he got over that fence, I was going to rip most of his face off with my fingernails." She shifted and recrossed her legs. "I guess he was . . . out of his mind."

"Beyond his mind," I said. "He was over into an area where his mind couldn't work any more."

"Then . . . my impersonation did what you wanted."

"Beyond my wildest dreams, Miss Merrimay. All I wanted to do was get him so rattled he'd make mistakes. I didn't hope for such a convenient arrest. They've got him now, and they ought to get a very interesting reaction when they let him read what the girl wrote. Meanwhile, I offer a steadying drink aboard the *Flush*."

"I'd like that," she said. "I hope my next acting job gets that big a reaction."

Once we were settled aboard in the lounge, the air-conditioners laboring to bring it back down to a lower setting, drinks in hand, our gear transferred from Merrimay Lane's car to our respective boats, Meyer said, "Something puzzles me, nought, nought, six and seven-eighths. That poisonous little chippy is going to keep mentioning your name at every opportunity. You are not entirely unknown to the local gestapo. And how do you expect to stay out of it?"

"Out of what? Nobody saw her in my stateroom. Do you think anybody on that boat will admit they can be bribed to let people stay aboard until customs has folded its tent and gone home? Miss Merrimay Lane, a client of a dear friend, met us both when customs had cleared us. We came back here. Who was the darkhaired girl who left off the confession and made the phone calls? I wouldn't have any idea. Oh, how did the blonde get my name? Hell, boys, I struck up an acquaintance yesterday afternoon on Bay Street and talked her into a friendly drink. Wouldn't you? We traded names. Mrs. Del Terry. But I didn't continue the acquaintance aboard ship, not after I got a good look at the shoulders on that guy. Boys, believe me, I never heard of any Tami Western in my life, or any Vangie. What I think, she's trying to smokescreen the issue. Maybe I look a little like the guy who met her at the boat and took off with her, and she's covering for him by giving you my name. Con man! Are you out of your mind?"

Merrimay put her empty glass down and stood up. "Dears, don't say it hasn't been interesting. But I have an afternoon date in Miami with some sweaty old leotards. I love your lovely money, and I love your generous little bonus. And it's good for the glands to get terrified once in a while. But most of all I love the luck. I love the way you showed up and got Uncle Jake to take a better look at me. And if I have to tell lies for you, I'll have the widest most innocent brown eyes you ever did see." She patted Meyer and kissed him on the forehead. I walked her out onto the stern deck, to the little gangplank that crosses over to the pier.

She put her hand lightly on my shoulder and studied me with intent brown eyes. "And you, McGee. If my luck starts to run bad, do you keep a fresh supply?"

"At all times."

She tilted her mouth up against mine, quite briefly, her lips soft and leaving an impression of coolness. "I might be by for some someday."

I watched her walk briskly toward her car, the red skirt swinging against good legs. She did not glance back.

Meyer surrendered the belt. I put the twenty-six thousand in my watery vault. Later, in the news stories, I found the information I wanted, the address of Powell Daniels' divorced wife and their twin fifteen-year-old sons. I wrapped up the money. I used a ruler to print the name and address. No handwriting expert in the world can make any identification of block letters, all caps, printed with a ruler. I sent it parcel post, special handling, from Miami's main post office.

And by then, of course, they had them all. Terry, Loyal,

Berga, Macklin, the Barntree woman and the Stusslund woman, and they were searching the continent from Hudson Bay to Acapulco for Walter Griffin. Macklin said Griff shoved Vangie into the speeding path of the stolen car, and that she was so terrified she was only semiconscious. Macklin had been driving the car. Nogs had given the order.

Drowners, Incorporated, was the name some reporter stuck on them. Despite all the frantic efforts of the tourist industry in the Broward Beach area to get it handled with the same emphasis as a parking ticket, the whole thing, as you will remember, was page one, prime time shrillness for day after day, with much editorializing about greed, callousness and the decay of moral standards.

Before the grand jury returned the indictments in record time, I was summoned up to the women's wing of the Broward Beach jail for a confrontation with the Stusslund woman. Though they'd had her only ten days, her discreet tan had faded to paste, and all the life had gone out of the hair of cream, so that it hung in dulled strands. She wore a baggy gray cotton dress without a belt and paper shower shoes. There were deep violet smudges under her eyes.

The sweet little kiddy-voice was unchanged. "Why did you *do* that to me! Why?"

"Do what? Buy you a drink in Nassau?"

We had a large interested audience. "Honey, *please!* You tricked me into writing the confession. Tell them! My God, tell them how it was, darling! You made promises! You were going to take me to Jersey."

"Wish I could help out, girlie. But I don't know what your angle is. It doesn't make any sense. I don't have a twin brother, and the last time I ever saw you, until right now, was in the ship's dining room. I don't see how it can do you any good trying to bring me into this. Either you did what you wrote down or you didn't."

"So it's going to be like that, you bastard?"

"It's going to be what happened, that's all."

First she made a pretty fair attempt to get her thumb-

nails into my eyes, but the matrons caught her and
held her in restraint. As they took her out, that fatty
little mouth opened into a round horror-hole. In a candy-
sweet chant she said words and phrases that seemed to
fume and smoke in the jail air, to give off a tangible
aroma of rot. She ejected the last few over her shoulder
as they dragged her out, and when the sound had faded,
some very professional officers of the law took out hand-
kerchiefs and mopped their faces.

On the Fourth of July I got Mcyer to take ten thousand
of what I had found in Vangie's kitchen ceiling. At first
he would have no part of it, but then after frowning
into space for half a minute, he suddenly agreed.

The next day he showed me a copy of something he
had pecked out on his typewriter, titled Meyer Mani-
festo. It was a stately mass of whereas, wherefore, and
be it resolved, and after I had sifted out the meat of it,
I discovered that he was putting the ten thousand into
a four and a half percent interest account, and that each
year he would draw out four hundred fifty dollars and
use it to finance the Meyer Festival on July Fourth
and such subsequent days as the Festival might continue
unabated. Invitations would be issued to convivial and
compatible persons, both of the permanent group and
the transient group, and it would be held upon a beach
area to be designated each year, the only stipulation
being that it would be a deserted beach accessible only
by boat. The theme of the Festival would be Booze,
Broads, Beer, Bonhomie, Bach, Blues and Rhythm, Bom-
bast, Blarney and Behavioral Psychology.

I guess he saw that I had to fake my pleasurable
approval. Things were getting flat and wistfully sour.

The smart money had it all figured out about the
Drowners. The best odds were that the State would hold
a cook-in for Terry and Loyal, and that Jane Adele Stusslund and Delilah Delberta Barntree would get life, as
would Macklin. And Emil "Nogs" Berga would get twenty
to life.

Somehow, I couldn't haul myself back up out of the

sours. I kept slipping further in. When that happens to you, there is no continuity of self-awareness, no frequent appraisals . . . just a little flash of uncomfortable illumination from time to time, and you turn it off quickly because you don't like the bright light.

I would see my hand pouring a C-cup of Plymouth over ice, and I'd take a sup of it, spilling a little, and in wiping my chin feel that it had been a little too long between shaves.

And then one morning I went beach-walking at three o'clock and looked up just in time to see one hell of a shooting star. It really whipped across there, fast, hot and bright. I admired it. An old chunk of iron, after noodling around out there for half a billion years, had come in hot and fast at eight miles a second, and had gladdened the mind of a dreary pygmy on a starlit beach.

Suddenly I felt disgusted with myself. What the hell was the use of taking my retirement in segments whenever I could afford one if I was going to slop around and groan and finger the sad textures of my immortal soul? As opposed to the psychotic, the neurotic *knows* two and two make four, but he can't stand it. I admired the patience of my friends for putting up with me the last few weeks. Vidge had soured me a little, and Vangie had dropped off the bridge and accelerated the process, and then I had really put the lid on it by trapping that dumb empty punchboard into a life sentence.

Why be gloomy because the woman supply had run bad for a time? If there was any truth in averages, it had to start getting good. But it certainly wasn't going to improve if I kept spooking around like a wounded violinist. The world was good, and it had been one hell of a shooting star.

At ten o'clock that same morning, while entertaining myself with as many choruses as I could remember of the lass who had her 'ead tooked underneath 'er arm, and putting on a little topside paint at the same time, I glanced down at the dock and saw Meyer staring up at me in vast astonishment.

"It isn't always exactly on key," I said, "but it's real loud."

"It is that. Yes indeed."

"Clamber aboard for a brew."

We drank them under the topside awning.

Meyer said, "With a few more years of practice, boy, you could work up to, real manic depression. I never know when you're going to come bounding out of the slump. Or why."

"Decided I was spoiling my retirement all to hell."

"You weren't doing mine any good."

"Meyer, let us round up a boatload of amiable clowns, jolly doxies, and old drinking friends and go bonk-chonkie bonk-chonkie up the Inland Waterway in this lush tub, visit old haunts, scare the sea birds, invent parlor games and outrage the shoredwellers. And, incidentally, regain our health, our clean young American good looks."

"McGee, the last time I came back I went to bed for a week."

"Let's try for ten days."

I heard the distant ringing of my phone, cursed it, decided finally to answer it.

A small forlorn voice I did not recognize said, "Travis?"

"Yes, dear."

"About that luck. How's the supply?"

The voice had been so dispirited and uncharacteristic I had not identified it until then. "Merrimay, unless I get rid of some, the supply is going to sink the boat. What's wrong?"

"Oh, I had to talk big. You know. And Uncle Jake got me a test. And I blew it. I came on like country ham. Old Rubberface herself. Actress! Ha! I don't want to face any of the gang I run with, and get patted on the head and told I'm still a great dancer. Travis, if maybe you could make up a sort of CARE package. Some of that luck, and a thick steak and red wine. . . . Maybe you're all sewed up?"

"And bring it to you at five-thirty?"

"Or five. I might not be any bundle of cheer, though." She sighed. "Got a pencil handy? Write down the address."

When I climbed back to the sundeck Meyer said, "I've made a tentative mental list of the passengers for this epic voyage. Let me check them out with you."

"Sure, Meyer."

After about six names he leaned and snapped his fingers in front of my face. "I get the curious feeling you aren't listening."

"They're *great* names. *Great,* Meyer. Who were they again?"

"Pierce, Fenner, Smith, Kidder, Beane and Goodbody," he said disgustedly and went home.

I think I sat right there for a long time.

Just smiling.

About the Author

JOHN D. MacDONALD, says *The New York Times,* "is a very good writer, not just a good 'mystery writer.' " His Travis McGee novels have established their hero as a modern-day Sam Spade and, along with MacDonald's more than 500 short stories and other bestselling novels—60 in all, including *Condominium* and *The Green Ripper*—have stamped their author as one of America's best all-round contemporary storytellers.